I0531602

Storylandia

The Wapshott Journal of Fiction

Issue 29

Storylandia, Issue 29, The Wapshott Journal of Fiction, ISSN 1947-5349, ISBN 978-1-942007-24-1 is published at intervals by the Wapshott Press, now a 501(c)(3) nonprofit, PO Box 31513, Los Angeles, California, 90031-0513, telephone 323-201-7147. All correspondence can be sent to The Wapshott Press, PO Box 31513, LA CA 90031-0513. Visit our website at www.WapshottPress.org to learn more. This work is copyright © 2019 by Storylandia. The Wapshott Journal of Fiction, Los Angeles, California. Copyright © 2018 Tom Larsen and is reprinted here with the copyright owner's permission.

Storylandia is always seeking quality original short stories, novelettes, and novellas. Please have a look at our submission guidelines at www.Storylandia.WapshottPress.org or email the editor at editor@wapshottpress.org

Donations happily accepted at donate.wapshottpress.org

Cover: Photo by Tom Larsen

"Humboldt" first appeared in Adelaide Literary Magazine - Spring 2017
"The Lip" first appeared in Philadelphia Stories Magazine - Fall 2009
"Well Connected" first appeared in Writes for All - Vol 2, Issue 6 - June 2012

Storylandia

The Wapshott Journal of Fiction

Founded in 2009

Issue 29, Spring 2019

Edited by Ginger Mayerson

Crime Spree and Other Stories
By Tom Larsen

Crime Spree
and Other Stories

by
Tom Larsen

BERNARDO

Take it from me. You can fall asleep on your feet, but sooner or later your knees will buckle. Happened plenty of times running presses over at Acme Press. It's a crazy feeling waking up like that and sometimes, for a second there, you don't know where the hell you are. Then it's back in a flash and you see it's so wrong for you. At least I did, which is why I quit.

Clever name, Acme, right? Believe me these guys were murder. The Donnelli brothers would screw you just to stay in shape and every guy there had gone a few rounds with them. Jack, the bulldog, throwing his arms around, smacking his head like he can't believe it. Believe it, Jack. Things go wrong all the time in a print shop. For what the Donnellis charge, customers expect the best. But I can tell you that's expecting too much.

Then there's Al. The "brains" of the family, a man with more tics than a cuckoo clock. Al's the excitable type. He has a degree in dentistry, but the histrionics make him unemployable. He's also gay; a bad combination in a Neanderthal trade. I liked to work him up into a lather then get all big and crazy so he'd think he'd crossed a line. If that's homophobic, so be it. Where I come from an asshole is an asshole.

Some days I'd get a long run, twenty, thirty thousand and an hour in that press would be running itself. Forget about shooting the breeze or catching a few scores in the paper. The Donnellis wanted their pound of flesh and that meant keeping your nose to the grindstone. So you pull a few sheets and you fiddle around and pretty soon you start to fade. Maybe you were up late or you had a few too many and you know you've got five more hours of standing around watching the clock, worrying about one stupid thing or another. It wears you out, I can tell you. Pretty soon the eyes are drooping and the noise seems to fade and then boom! Your knees give out. It's a funny thing to see unless your name's Donnelli.

Most guys I've worked with would kill to get out of the business, but with families and the time put in it's hard to walk away. I did and I ain't looking back. People don't realize the pressure printers are under. One little mistake and it's ten grand down the shitter. The halftones are reversed or phone number's scrambled and it's NFG (No Fucking Good)! Skids of product no one can use and you get to run the whole thing over. Not your fault, maybe, but you made it irreversible. Shit didn't run itself, dude. That's not even considering the stuff that is your fault, you backed it up wrong or it's crooked or it offset or a million other things. Every printer I know drinks too much and most have an ex-wife or two on retainer.

The schmoozing thing really bugged me. You work with guys every day, but if you can't talk to them you can't get to know them. And I'm the kind of guy; if I don't know you I generally don't like you. It drives my wife nuts but it's something I can't change. To me everybody's a blowhard until they prove different. So Acme was basically a shop full of grumblers who hated the boss and kept their distance. I was there ten years. I spent more time with those shmos than I did with my family, but I didn't know where one of them lived. Take it from me it wasn't natural.

So OK, I may be slow to warm, but I'm no sociopath. I've worked in places where the crew was as tight as a TV family. Worked together, played together, married each other, got divorced. I still have friends I haven't worked with in twenty years. So when I say Acme was unnatural, I hold myself apart from it. From my first day I could see what the problem was. I was fifteen years younger than the next guy and I was pushing forty. A few decades running presses will knock the snot out of you and suddenly the old pension's so close you can taste it. So the job sucks. It's almost over. Get through the fucking day.

None of this was lost on the Donnellis.

Not that we NEVER talked to each other. Some days there'd be nothing else to do or you'd run into one of them in the mall and you'd have a few words, mostly about the boss. The Donnellis did this or said that, and always some big talk about getting even, dropping a wrench between cylinders or tipping off OSHA. The longer I was there, the worse it got.

OK, that's my fault. You don't like the job you get another or you do something to change it. But the only thing worse than working is not working. I've been there often enough. Sit around the house driving the old lady nuts, Try finding work when you really need it, especially when you've been around and expect to earn a decent wage. The trades have dried up here and everywhere, so you hold on to what you got. You might not like it, but you shut up and take it. Or you walk away and hope for the best.

~

When I think back to how I got into printing it's almost comical. I'd been to college a few years, but what I got out of it was either sexually transmitted or drug related. This was back in the seventies when a career was what your dad had and your dad was a loser. Guys I know now are surprised when they hear I went to college. Most of them came from working class where higher education meant finishing twelfth grade. My dad made a good living, but he was convinced a degree would have made him and he was probably right. From the time we could listen he harped on college, drummed it in our heads until we hated to be around him. He must have thought we'd go along just to shut him up and for a while we did. Then the old man died and in the end not a one of us could hack it.

I knew I'd have to get a job, but back then I was pretty particular. No suit and tie, no sucking up, no working my way up the ladder, not me. I wanted a skill that would let me be mobile. Not a career but an occupation, something to pay the bills while I figured out how to make my mark. I was leafing through the phone book to see what was out there and when I got to the P's my fate was sealed. If I'd given it any thought I would have seen the limitations, advancement, for instance. Once you're the printer there's nowhere to go. OK, foreman, maybe, but that's a suck up job and the pay is only slightly higher. So where does that leave you? You're never going to own the place, not on a printer's paycheck. It took me a while to see my mistake. What's good money when you're 20 is peanuts when you're hitting 50 and your kid brother just bought a place in Pompano.

Acme Press is a real shit hole, I can tell you. Funny thing is I loved the building, a hundred years old, easy, with high ceilings and big windows facing out on the city. You couldn't really see through them, what with fifty years of grime, but some mornings those shafts of light were as soft and warm as an old flannel shirt. The place was a monument to industry, one of those brick monoliths that take up the whole block, covered in graffiti, rust belt down to the dumb waiters and the wood brick floors. From a distance the building looked haunted and up close it could break your heart. I got to like going to work in a scary looking place. When I left for the last time I pried up one of those wood bricks and took it home with me.

It was the mouse that pushed me over the edge. Being old and semi permeable, the building was a haven for the lower life forms. Rats, bats, pigeons, the odd crackhead, and bugs! Holy Jesus! Horrible things with fat, hairy bodies and more legs than they'd ever need. And not shy about making an appearance either. You'd be smoothing ink into the fountain and all of a sudden something would catch your eye, moving fast over the wooden bricks, slipping under your press and not coming out. Gave me the willies, I can tell you. One time Big Lenny crushed three toes stomping one of them on his shoe, a truly funny thing to see.

So the place was a dump and a few bugs weren't gonna make much difference. But then Jack brought his wife in to work the phones and the Godzilla of bugs took up in the file cabinet. Like she'd found a head in there from the way she went off. Jack called in an exterminator, skinny guy with a spray wand. He went along the floors and into the corners, nodding and smiling like we were all in the same boat. The smile of a man who expected more from life, but believed, in his way, he was making a difference. We watched him angling around work tables, squeezing into places no one ever thought to go, spritzing every cranny with God knows what. We stood there smirking in the time-honored way of slightly skilled men lording it over slightly less skilled men.

"What the hell is he so happy about?" Big Lenny wondered.

I shrugged. "Maybe he's drunk."

"What kind of job is that for a grown man?" Owens shook his head. "I stopped killing bugs when I was six."

"The kind you have right before you throw yourself off the bridge." Lenny snickered.

Owens sucked his teeth reflectively. "It's the uniform, with the name above the pocket. That's where I draw the line."

I looked down at my own uniform, then to Lenny's, then Owens.

"OK, but ours are cool," Owens said in all seriousness, glancing at the name above his pocket, something long and Polish. "It's like a disguise or something."

"The bow tie," Lenny muttered, almost to himself. "That's where I draw the fucking line,"

The guy wasn't wearing a bow tie but Owens and I never let on.

I first saw the mouse when I was cleaning up to go home. Things were slow and I was drawing it out. It's the slow days that never end. I was digging through a box of parts when I spotted him under my workbench. There was something wrong with his leg or back, some deformity or old injury. It didn't seem to bother him much, but it made me wonder what was in that spray wand.

I watched him poke around an old gripper

assembly, nosing along as the press pounded a few feet away. I figured he was hungry so I tossed a few donut crumbs over. The crumbs startled him and he darted off, but a few minutes later he was back, sniffing the length of chain, sniffing the crumbs then sniffing all the other crap down there. Marking things for later, or so I thought. But the crumbs were there the next day and may be there still for all I know.

He'd only show when the press was cranking. Maybe with the noise he thought I couldn't see him, or maybe with the noise he couldn't see me. What I know about mice is they're smaller than you'd think. I'll admit I looked forward to seeing him. What the hell, he was cute. I thought about what it must be like creeping around the old plant at night, not so bad, I suppose. There's heat and water and plenty of junk to hide in. You can pass in or out in a million places and there are two fast food dumpsters in the alley out back. A mouse might spend his whole life in here, generation after generation passing down the secrets.

How long does a mouse live anyway? My guess is not too long. Almost anything will kill you and tunneling through garbage all day can't be healthy. To me mice seem super skittish and I'm thinking lots of them die of fright. When you're that small and that defenseless you know your place on the food chain. Low man must be stressful. When your number's up you blow all the gaskets.

"Got a little mouse at the job," I told the wife over supper.

"A mouse? You sure it's not a rat?"

"Believe me, you wouldn't get them confused. This guy's tiny," I held my finger and thumb a mouse length apart.

"Better kill it."

"What do you mean? I like him."

"Mice have fleas and fleas carry diseases. Remember that show on PBS?"

"I'm not going to kill him. He's a friend of mine."

"OK."

"His name is Bernardo."

"Bernardo."

"Right."

I was running Safeco's annual report when the pest control guy showed up again. Watching him, I couldn't help wondering what it was like, exterminating for a living. The day's work measured in small-scale carnage, genocide, when you think about it. Sure it's bugs and vermin, but they were living and now they're dead. Where he goes tiny organs dissolve, synapses misfire, little limbs and segments wriggle their last. Whole populations, countless thousands wiped out in the wave of his wand. The few who survive breed a stronger strain, immune to the toxins, then stronger toxins.

There must be consequences to his line of work.

He made his way toward me and smiled his big smile. I gave him a nod and motioned him over.

"Hiya," he studied the thumping Heidleberg, eyes wide at the wonder of it. "Boy, ain't she something,"

I glanced back then led him off a few paces. He stood solemn and trusting, the wand at his side. My smile was barely menacing.

"Listen," I checked his shirt, "Bert, can I ask you a favor?"

"Sure. What's the problem, uh..." he squinted at mine. "Pinky?"

"The problem is I got a thing about, you know," I pointed to the canister.

"Oh...?"

"Look, I know you got a job to do, but..." I ran a hand over my face for effect. "You remember Agent Orange, right Bert?"

"You mean?"

"That's right. Pleku, it's not something I like to talk about."

"No hey, I understand."

"I mean most of the time I feel OK, OK?"

He looked down at the wand, the canister. I did the hand over the face thing again.

"Whaddya say Bert, can we make a deal? Do what you have to do, but can we skip around here. Just, you know," I gestured to the immediate area.

"I gotta tell you though, this stuff has been tested by every underwriter in the business. Seriously. The chances of you..."

I let the smile sag.

"Uh," he looked around as if someone could hear us. "See, I'd have to check with the owner."

"Bert, look at me," the smile gone now, replaced by a world-weary grimace. "I didn't ask to be sterilized. You know what I'm saying? I didn't sign on to have my liver pickled or my brain cells scrambled."

"Oh my Lord."

"You ever get night sweats, Bert? How about it?"

"Gee no, but–"

"C'mere," I drew him to me. "Answer me this. Did you ever catch yourself staring into space trying to remember your kid's name?"

Bert turned deathly pale.

"It's not that much to ask, my friend. Not that you owe me a thing."

"OK," his eyes didn't quite meet mine. "It's against company policy, but you're right. Jesus. We've done enough to you already."

"You're a stand-up guy Bert. I won't forget it," I clapped him on the shoulder and sent him on his murdering way.

Not that it would make any difference. Hosed down the way it was the building had to be toxic. The mouse came around now and then but he probably combed the whole building, soaking up poisons like a sponge. Spray day had to be the worst, though, a fresh coating of lethal substance settling over. Surely he can smell it and feel it in his eyes. Hey, I'm no animal rights nut, but I'm no sadist either. The nature of pain is to be painful. For the creepy-crawlies you can overlook it, but a crippled little mouse? I don't know. It didn't sit right.

I didn't see Bernardo for a while. I went on vacation and when I came back, the shop had been painted. They'd covered the presses, moved everything else away from the walls and sprayed the whole place. The color, a slight variation on the old toothpaste green made it feel more like prison than it did before. I couldn't see why the Donellis would bother, but then Lenny told me they'd gotten a "deal" on it, some poor schlub working off his business card debt, if I had to bet. He said Jack's wife had nagged him into it, but brother Al was refusing to kick in. I don't know why this cheered me up but it did. Something about the brothers going at it always made my day.

The schlub's crew really botched the job. Paint had hardened into lumps and dribbles. The floor was rimmed inches deep and the windows and fixtures had taken a dusting. Anything that hadn't been moved had been painted over, including the arm of my chair and my poster of Westbrook breaking a long one. Paint was everywhere. I could still smell it.

Shortly after lunch something moved under my workbench. Crouching down I saw a gob of green inching along the green gripper assembly. The mouse was crusted in paint, just his legs moving under a green shell. It didn't look like collateral damage either. Someone had zeroed in. On top of everything else Bernardo had been gang painted.

Enough was enough. Those Donellis always struck me as sadists, but this was way beyond the pale. I scrunched down on my hands and knees and poked around with the dolly hook. Bernardo rolled out and I scooped him up. Oh man, it was pitiful. One of his legs was bound up inside and his eyes had been painted shut! I took him to the sink but it was hopeless. I could pick away bits and pieces but only a solvent would do the job. And then I noticed he wasn't moving anymore. I touched his little head but it just rolled back in the collar of paint. I'd been careful with the water so he couldn't have drowned. I might have scared him too much, but I had to do something. I was sure he was dead, but I laid him on workbench and checked on him all morning to be sure. Little guy never moved a muscle. Just before noon I walked into the lunchroom, opened the refrigerator, popped a Tupperware top and buried Bernardo in Jack's lasagna. That done I cleaned out my locker, pried up a floor brick and took the el home.

CRIME SPREE

We were too smart to get caught. That's what we told ourselves. We knew morons who were making out and nitwits who could buy and sell us. Oh sure, once in a while one of them would serve a stretch, but not for so long you'd even notice. Crime paid pretty well from what we could see.

And working a hustle was so easy in those days. No computers, no high tech security, not much to separate you from their money. Take checking accounts, for instance. The most sophisticated system they had back then was a thing called Telecheck. The store would call a number, the number would call the bank and the bank would confirm that you had the funds. Of course if it was the weekend no checks would clear so your balance came up the same every time. As long as you didn't cross that line on any one purchase, the check would be OK'd. Write a dozen checks for the full amount or less and every one would sail right through.

Candy from a baby, am I right?

Andree wasn't keen on the idea at first. We'd kept our noses clean over the years and lived a pretty conventional life. Oh, I'd sell a little weed sometimes but mostly I just smoked it. Andree had a scrip or two, but we were lightweights compared to most, a couple of working stiffs, paying taxes and getting the shaft.

"I think we should go for it," I nagged her.

Andree gave me her 'get serious' look. "Let me ask you something. Do you think Allan Bateman would consider something like this?"

Allan was my one friend from the neighborhood who turned out OK. More than OK when you threw in the house in Seaside and the Aprils in Paris. Andree played the Allan card whenever I talked nonsense. Usually it worked, but I'd seen my guy recently and he was driving a car that cost more than my condo!

"Al has the knack," I explained for the hundredth time. "He can spin straw into gold, so what? Does that mean the rest of us have to eke out a living?"

"It's not that. He would look at the downside. The downside of a felony is jail. End of pipedream."

Pipedream. That was her dad's word. He used it to describe anything I came up with in the way of a future for his daughter. Mercifully, he's dead now but the word lives on.

"The chances of getting caught are slim and none."

That was *my* dad talking, usually in regards to my prospects in life. The old boys were much the same on that score.

"OK, mastermind" Andree folded her arms. "Tell me again how you'd do this."

"OK, first I get some fake ID."

"Impersonation, fraud."

"Then I open a checking account."

"Forgery, racketeering."

"How is that racketeering? It's a just a checking account!"

"It's a racket! What do you think, they'll go easy on you just because you have an apostrophe in your name?"

O'Keefe, that's me. In her heart Andree loves that apostrophe, the little oomph it gives her first name? She had a point, though. It's been a century or two since the micks ran the bunco squad, if there still was a bunco squad.

"Listen to you!" I tried to sound miffed. "If I go to the precinct house and make a full confession maybe, just maybe I take a fall. We're talking sleight of hand here, not smash and grab!"

"Don't snow me Vic. You can always talk the game but we both know better."

"What about your brother? He beat the finance company and he couldn't read a bus schedule."

"You can't count on people being stupid."

"Yes. You can."

I knew I could make her come around. Andree had her eye on a tiger maple chest for the living room and if I could convince her it could be hers, the means would be easier to swallow. It wouldn't be HER ass, after all, worst-case scenario she'd be rid of me for a while, though I didn't want to stress that point. The condo and the car were already in her name and no one could take the apostrophe from her.

I'm not her first husband, it goes without saying.

First thing, fake ID. Back then they had a state issued card that looked just like a driver's license if you ignored the words 'This Is Not A License To Drive' lettered in yellow across the top. Didn't matter. ID was ID. Hey, people who don't drive have to cash checks too. Getting the card was as easy as covering the names and dates on my birth certificate, making a copy and filling in the spaces with different names and dates. I picked Wilson, keeping my first name to avoid slip-ups.

Setting Wilson up with an address was a little

stickier. No post office would accept my bogus birth certificate. But for a nominal fee the Edgewood Arms was glad to oblige, lodgings by the month, week, or hour, according to the Yellow Pages. It took a few calls and a trip across town, but a flophouse mail drop seemed so right. I filled in the address on the ID application, had my picture taken and in a matter of weeks I had my nom de guerre.

Andree was not impressed.

"Who's Victor Wilson?" she waved the ID card in my face. "And where's 11A, Edgewood Arms?"

"That's suite 11A."

"You know you're really getting on my nerves with this. Why can't I have a normal husband with the normal screws loose?"

"I'm taking money from a bank! It's a victimless crime!"

"Oh sure, in the unlikely event you get away with it."

"You're so negative," I tossed her one of her own lines. "I'd think you'd want to support me on this."

"Aiding and abetting."

"Admit it. You never thought I'd get this far. Baby, I got the freaking ID!"

"Big deal. What about a work history? What about a social security card?" she reeled off a half dozen more. "Banks care about that stuff, you know."

"You're wrong, Andree. Banks don't care about that stuff. Give them a deposit and they'll open an account. Jake the bookie has overdraft protection, for Christ sake. That's like giving a diabetic the key to the cookie jar."

A sloppy analogy, but then she wasn't listening anyway.

"What do you use for a deposit, huh? And how

do you get it back once the shit hits the fan?" Her old man again. Shit hitting fans was a theme with him.

"Let me worry about that, will you? This will be a piece of cake," my dad, on *his* pipedreams.

Amazingly, it went just like I said it would. I picked a bank in the burbs for the obvious reasons. Nobody asked any questions and no one had the slightest doubt I was who I said I was. I opened the account with a six hundred dollar advance from Andree's Visa card and just like that we were in business.

But before diving in, I wanted to check in with Herbie for some professional insight. Herbie, my dope connection, is a practicing fence and recovering crackhead. We did two years in juvee together and I trust him as much as I trust anyone. A good man, Herbie, had a rap sheet that read like a telephone book, but that's the angle I was looking for. If there was a way to fuck up, Herbie would know about it. Took me a few days but I finally tracked him down on the basketball court at the rec center.

"Too white collar for me, pissant," he nailed a rainbow jumper from half court. "Your basic entrepreneur sees a black man flash a check and all the red flags go up."

"What about a disguise?" I faked left and hooked right. Herbie slammed it back in my face.

"What for, brother?" he laughed that lazy laugh. "You already impersonating a real human being."

"But what if somebody recognizes me?" I rubbed the welt on my forehead. "I'm thinking disguise. Maybe a fake beard or something."

"You always were a little freaky, pissant."

With Herbie everything comes with a measure of abuse. We'd known each other for a lot of years, but

I don't think he's ever called me by name.

I faked left and drove right. Herbie was waiting for me.

"OK, forget the disguise" I ran the ball down and checked it for bloodstains. "How about unloading the stuff. You can take care of it?"

He blew by me for a windmill slam. "Think about it, pissant. At ten cents on the dollar you'd be better off just getting what you need."

"But that sorta takes the edge off of knowing a fence, doesn't it?"

"Hey man, my brother's a plumber. That don't mean he's been in my toilet."

So much for criminal expertise.

I did my homework. To make sure the Telecheck system worked like I said it did, I put a few things on my own account. I hit the malls on a Saturday. None of my purchases exceeded my tiny balance, but together they nearly tripled it. Not a problem. The salesmen made the calls and got the OK's. Then I tried some items that were over my limit and sure enough, Telecheck nixed the deal. Twice in a row I'd called it right. Reason enough to give it up, Andree would say.

It was time to get her going on this.

"I was over at the Antique Barn. They still have that chest, you liked"

"Don't snow me, Victor," she held a hand up. "You're gonna do what you're gonna do so skip the song and dance."

Victor. Not good. It worried me to think she could see right through me, but then ten years together give you a sense of things. Lucky for me that stuff works both ways.

~

"... and bath towels. Plush ones like they have in the hotels," Andree underlined the "plush". We were in McGlinchey's and the vodka tonics were working their magic. "Oh, and new pots, the old ones are disgusting."

It took some work but the tiger maple chest was the clincher. Sometimes all you have to do is sow the seed.

"What about that rug in the hallway?" I pushed some more buttons.

"And new curtains! I saw some in Wannamakers that would be perfect for the kitchen."

What the hell, Herbie was probably right. Get what you need while you have the chance. Besides, there were plenty of checks to go around.

"What kind of TV can you get for six bills?" I wondered.

"A Tinitron. With one remote that works everything."

"You checked?" I tried to sound surprised.

"Hey, if you're gonna throw it all away you might as well have something to show for it."

"Atta girl."

One thing still bothered me. In the unlikely event we had to make a run for it, I didn't want it to be in our own car. Most of the rental agencies wanted a credit card, but another go at the Yellow Pages turned up Charlie's Rent a Wreck. Low budget, high mileage, no questions asked.

"This here one's only twelve years old. One previous owner," Charlie circled the Country Squire.

Andree leaned inside. "It's got 200,000 miles on it. Jesus, the poor guy musta lived behind the wheel."

"Fuller brush man. Thirty years on the road and not so much as a speeding ticket," Charlie laid it on.

"What about the van?" I pointed to a dented Econoline with a primered front end.

"I'm kinda partial to the wagon, here," Charlie picked at some rust on the quarter panel. "Don't build 'em like this anymore."

"Thing is, we're moving so we need something roomy," I told him.

"You don't want that van then, Damn things fulla tars."

"Tars?"

"He means tires," Andree translated.

"Nothing good," Charlie shrugged. "Old retreads and such. I tried to get rid of 'em but you can't dump tars no more, since that far under the freeway."

"He means–"

"I know what he means."

"Besides, you can fit just as much or more in this old Squar."

The wagon was a boat all right. We'd have to hold off on a couple of things but the bulk of the list was within cargo range.

"How much for the weekend?"

Charlie grinned, "You two are in luck. We just started a weekend special, thirty samolies, plus a deposit."

"That's dol–"

"You take a check?"

"Personal check?" I could hear the old boy's wheels turning. "Let me make a call on that and we'll see what we can do. Oh. I'll need your driver's license."

I filled out a check and handed him the ID. Charlie checked the card.

"Says here this ain't no driver's license," he flipped it over like that might clear things up.

"Shit! I must have left it in my other wallet."

I slapped at my pockets. "That card's valid though. They'll OK the check."

"You're not trying to pull a fast one on me, are you?" Charlie's smile was a dental nightmare. "See, cause it makes me nervous, young couple like you rentin' a heap like this. What do you want the car for anyway?"

"Like I said, we're moving,"

"That's OK, I don't want to know," he waved me off and turned for the office. "Long as the check's good we can finagle the rest."

"You're a good man Charlie. I'll make it up to you."

The old man hacked up a laugh. "I'm thinking a man with two wallets will promise you anything."

I was getting a real good feeling about this.

We took the bus to Rent a Wreck the following Friday. The Country Squire looked bigger than I remembered and we nearly clipped a gatepost pulling out of the lot.

"You look like an idiot. You know that, don't you?" Andree called over from across the seat.

"What? I think it changes my look completely," I double-checked the moustache in the mirror.

"It's not even touching your face at the ends. It's like you stapled it to your lip."

"You notice because you know it's not real. No one else will even see it."

"But it won't match the picture on the ID card."

"So, maybe I just grew it."

"I'm just saying, you walk into a store with a shrubbery on you lip and people tend to notice."

"Just humor me, OK?"

The gas gauge read half a tank but to play it safe I pulled in the station for a fill up. The kid at the pumps wasn't going for it.

"At's a fake moustache ain't it?"

"Just fill the tank, will ya?"

"You gotta unlock the flap."

I felt around the floor, pushing buttons and pulling levers. The seat whirred and the back came forward, folding me into the steering wheel. The switches on the door worked a window apiece and the handle under the dash popped the front hood. The kid just looked at me, holding the nozzle like he might have to use it. The markings on the dashboard controls had worn away so I pushed, pulled and switched them all. Wipers, washers, flashers, all worked like a charm.

"At's a rug, too, ain't it?" the kid snickered.

"Know what?" I peeled off the moustache and tossed it out the window. "Forget the gas."

The mall was a new one in the Northeast. I had a little trouble finding it, which is like having trouble finding the Atlantic in Atlantic City. OK, Andree's line, but close to the truth. The parking lot stretched farther than the eye could see. I cruised around for a spot close in, but the only ones open wouldn't fit half the Squire.

"There's somebody leaving," Andree nodded to a fat guy shuffling across the blacktop. I fell in behind him, moving at a crawl.

"So we get the bikes already assembled, got it?" I inched up half a car length.

"But they'll take up so much room."

"I'm no mechanic, baby."

"My dad could take my bike apart and put it together with one hand tied behind his back."

"That's funny. My take was your dad couldn't find his ass with BOTH hands tied behind his back."

"What's this thing you have about my father's ass?"

The fat guy cut between two cars and over a row.

I gunned the Squire around and up the other side.

"Where the hell did he go?"

"There's somebody else," Andree pointed to an old black woman loading bags in her trunk. Three rows away, but a half-mile in cutbacks.

"Hurry!" Andree jabbed me in the knee.

"In a mall? You know how many kids live here?"

By some miracle she was still at it when we drove up minutes later. From where we sat you could see rolls of flesh bunched above her old lady stockings. When the last bag was in just right she pulled something out and placed it in a second bag. Then she took two things out of the second bag and put one each in bags one and three. That was no better so she switched two of the bags around. I gave the horn a poke. Bip!

"Don't you honk that horn at me," she said without turning. "You be an old man before I move this car, you pasty face motherfucker."

"Maybe we can find something else," Andree pointed to empty stretch near the curvature of the earth. I put the Squire in gear.

The mall smelled of paint and industrial carpeting. A third of the stores weren't open yet and the ones that were had a slapdash feel. Still, the place was packed. They had a guy on stilts passing fliers in the atrium and a manic clown to make the kids cry. An hour since the doors opened and somebody had already puked on the escalator.

"This can't be real," I took a long look around. "They're piping in Herb Alpert."

"What's the difference?"

"In the mall? That's like a Doors soundtrack to a Viet Nam movie. Something bad has to happen."

"Look, there's Macy's," Andree pulled ahead.

Something about the way she moved told me I was losing control.

"Oh, this would go perfect with my new shoes," she checked a price tag in the mid three figures. "And it's on sale!"

"I didn't see slinky black dress on the list."

"Thirty percent off! Cough it up mastermind."

The girl at the register studied the photo on my ID.

"Well that's a coincidence," her eyes darted from the picture to me. "You're wearing the same shirt."

"Huh, Whaddya know?"

Hardly coincidence, dearie, more a last minute concession to the stupid moustache. If the faces didn't match at least I would be wearing Wilson's clothes.

"Let me just verify this and you're good to go," she held up my check like exhibit A.

"Oh man, I have to pee," Andree clutched at my arm as the sales girl made the call. It took a bit longer than expected, but she soon returned with a chipper smile.

"Will there be anything else for you today?" she pushed my card across the counter.

"No, I don't think–"

"How much is this paisley scarf?" Andree fingered one of a dozen.

"That's $90."

"We'll take it... and these two... three."

"Oh my God, you were right!" she practically danced down the concourse. "It's like a dream come true!"

"Cool it, will you? This place is probably crawling with security. Here, let's try this one." I steered her into an electronics outlet. A thousand components flashed triple zeroes as three saleschildren converged.

"How can I help you?" a little porker cut them off at mid counter.

"We need a new stereo," I nodded to a shelf full. "Something with all the bells and whistles."

"We have a full line of tuners and receivers," he led us along, gesturing as if it scarcely mattered. "Your brand names, your imports. Did you have a particular unit in mind?"

"Your $600 unit," I checked the names for something recognizable.

"With one remote that works everything," Andree added.

"All our tuners have full capability. How about a Hitachi?" he pointed to a finger smudged floor model. "This baby will do everything but feed the cat."

"Sold," I whipped out my checkbook.

"Excellent!" he signaled to a stock boy thrice his age. "I just purchased one myself. The multi-functional menu display is a real nice feature. Now then, can I interest you in something else? A set of new speakers?"

"Just the receiver."

"Tape deck? VCR?"

"Just the receiver."

"Do you have Trinitrons?" Andree had to ask.

"Ah, we do indeed." Salesboy herded us over to a wall of TVs, all shapes and sizes, Oprah times fifty at least.

"This is our most popular video item," Salesboy draped an arm over a mid-size Oprah. "In fact, we may be temporarily out of them. At the opening they were flying off the shelf."

"Does it come in any other color?" Andree cocked her head.

Salesboy smiled sadly, "I'm afraid basic black is

the industry standard."

"How about white?"

He looked to me, but the kid was on his own here.

"I could check," he headed off in a low waddle. I waited until he was out of earshot before making my case.

"What are you doing, Andree? The TV alone is over the limit."

"You should have used a bigger deposit."

I held my tongue. Her credit card statement wouldn't come for a week yet.

"Besides, we don't have to buy here," she reached over and switched stations. "It'll give us a basis for comparison."

The out of synch Trinitron showed a golfer poised to make a putt. The crowd rimmed around a sand trap, the announcers falling silent. The golfer stood still as a statue, only his hat moving as he checked the flag, then the ball, then the flag...

"What's wrong?" Andree leaned in closer.

"I think he's stuck."

Sure enough, the man couldn't pull the trigger. A full minute passed. Clouds drifted over the green. A paper wrapper skittered left to right. The camera seemed to tremble under the strain.

I grabbed Andree's arm. "Here comes Spanky."

"Wait. I want to see what happens."

What happened was nothing. The camera continued to roll but the fucking guy was paralyzed. We watched until our boy arrived then the three of us watched together. A pair of seagulls sauntered into the picture and the wrapper blew back the way it came. When they finally broke for commercials the air seemed to go out of the showroom.

"Sir?" Spanky's forehead was speckled in sweat. "I hate to tell you this, but both items are out of stock at the moment."

"OK, give me whatever you got."

"I'm afraid we're pretty much out of everything. There was a problem with delivery, new store and all."

I folded my arms to keep from throttling him. "You knew this going in, didn't you fatso?"

He blushed brightly, but held his ground.

"Sir, we've got everything on back order. The truck should be here on Wednesday. Free delivery, it goes without saying."

"Wednesday!" I checked my watch. We'd wasted an hour.

The flat tire took another twenty minutes. By the time we were on the road again my shirt was sweat soaked and my fingers were black.

"I mean the kid was what? Fifteen?" Andree kept at me about the sales guy. "You know, you can be a real bully at times."

"Come on, the kid played me like a violin."

"You didn't have to make him cry!"

"Look, we gotta concentrate. There's a time element involved here."

I watched the blood drain from Andree's face. "Stop the car, we have to go back."

"Go back?"

"I left the dress in the stereo store. FUCK! FUCK! FUCK!" she pounded the dash until the glove box flipped open.

"There's no going back, baby," I glared at her. "They see us coming they call the cops."

"No, I'll go in. I can reason with them."

"Forget it. We keep going," I eased up as taillights

flickered ahead. Off to the side red lights were flashing.

"What now?" Andree groaned.

"Aww look at this! I can see the fucking mall from here."

The jam up spread across three lanes. I toed the brake and the Squire squealed like a Septa bus.

It was nearly four by the time they cleared the wreckage. We squeezed through, drove a mile then cued up at the line for the Plymouth Meeting Mall exit. Forty minutes later we were in. I parked as close as I could, a short cab ride at most.

By now we were barely on speaking terms. I don't know what it is in men that make them blame their wives for everything, but whatever it is, I've got it. Royal bastard, that's me. Andree's girlfriends all say she's lucky to have me, but what they know about luck you could fit in a thimble. Without Andree I'd be just like they are, lonely, bitter, much divorced. At my worst, their ex's couldn't touch me.

"The way it fits together, 'jackknifed tractor trailer', like a snazzy new truck line," I muttered, as if to myself. "And how come WHEN they jackknife they're just long enough to block the whole interstate? Coincidence...? I think not."

"Please God, make him stop," Andree rolled her eyes to the heavens.

"Oh that's rich. Tell you something, I wish there was a God. You know what? I'd break his fucking nose."

"Just for five minutes, Jesus. That's all I ask."

"It just kills me. You know what this is like? It's like a blind man with 48 hours to see but nobody knows how to turn on the fucking lights! It's like–"

"Strike him dead if you must, Lord, but please..."

~

The bikes were a breeze. Keith, the salesman knew more about cycling than selling so we gave him all the rope he needed. You could hear the excitement in his voice when we got to the racers and a catch in his throat as he called up his glory days, the prep school trophies, tracing the route of the Tour de France. We settled on a pair of Pirellis, factory assembled. Keith was so thrilled, I thought he'd pay for them himself.

We stashed the bikes in the Squire and hustled back for more. Stuff for the bathroom, stuff for the bedroom, stuff we needed like a hole in the head. A popcorn popper, a pasta maker, a mini refrigerator, one of those wave machines, future shower and wedding gifts all. I don't know, when it's all free your needs seem many. Andree concentrated on essentials, new lamps, gardening tool, six cases of assorted wines. Her shopping skills were sharper than mine but I did my bit, carting off her booty with a good-natured grunt. My style was more all over the place. A box of ratchets I'd never open, new skis to hang in the basement, golf clubs and fishing gear, should I ever take them up. There's a rhythm to marathon shopping and we soon found ourselves falling into it. A casual entrance, a bit of indecision, an afterthought or two and boom! We were gone.

It took a good bit of rearranging, but in four trips the Squire was loaded.

"You forgot that," Andree pointed to the mini fridge behind me.

"aaaAAH Jesus Christ! Why didn't you say something sooner?"

She gave me that crushed scrotum look, with the hand on the hips and the foot tap going. "I don't know. Maybe I thought if I waited long enough you'd have a stroke."

"That's not funny."

"Sorry..." the eyes narrowed, "ummmm, maybe I couldn't think of the words," she conked herself on the head. "I don't know. I got gaps."

I gave a grunt. "How about the old standby 'I did, but you don't remember'. Or even better, 'I'm glad it doesn't fit. I really hated it'."

"Those, too."

"Come on. Let's go."

"We can't just leave it here."

"It won't fit. Forget about it."

"Good. I really hated it."

That first day really took it out of us. By the time we got home and unloaded, we could barely lift our vodka tonics. Six trips each up three flights then down a long hallway will do that to you. We didn't have the strength to put things away so it just piled up in the middle of the room. New stuff, ain't it pretty?

"It makes me nuts, that dress," Andree said, not for the first time.

"Baby, all this loot and you're worried about a dress? Tomorrow we'll get twenty dresses."

"It just grates on me. I loved that dress. Everything I really love I lose."

"Come on," I gestured to the pile. "How can you lose a Cuisinart?"

"To just walk off and leave it with that imbecile!"

"Ah hell, Skippy wasn't that bad."

"I thought it was Spanky."

"Whatever it was he'll hate it at sixty."

"And my scarves! I already had an outfit picked out for each one."

"Look, we were lucky to get anything. That wreck could have hung us up for days."

~

We studied the pile again over breakfast. The stuff didn't look ours yet. We didn't know the quirks and design flaws, hadn't yet discovered the defects or missing pieces. In time we'd use it up and throw it away, but for now it was all new and all ours.

"If I had a camera I'd take a picture of it," I framed the pile with my fingers.

"Camera," Andree aimed her finger at me. "Put it on the list."

"Cam-*corder*. Oh, and a cordless drill."

"For what?"

"I don't know. Drilling situations."

"I'm getting a whole new wardrobe. I can't believe I get to say that in my lifetime."

I cleared the dishes and poured two shots to soothe the nerves.

"Mazel tov!" we hailed each other and sallied forth.

Day two was a romp. Once we'd shit-canned indecision there was no stopping us. Andree snookered every shoe store in sight while I saw more dressing rooms than a backstage groupie. It was work, I can tell you. Try taking your shoes and pants off a few dozen times and you'll have some idea. At the same time it was exhilarating. We were cranked up and zeroed in. We were serious consumers on an all-consuming quest. Conditions couldn't have been better. Stores were stocked with the latest styles and sales staffs were quick and courteous. Like shooting cats in a barrel, as my dad would say.

Our last stop was the Antique Barn just before the bridge to Jersey. We filled the tiger maple chest with shoes and wedged it between the trash compactor and the gas grill.

"You folks sure been busy," antique guy looked

over our loot.

"We Wilson's come from hardy shopping stock," Andree assured him.

"Used to have me one of these," he ran a hand over the Squire's front fender. "Fine vehicle, as I recall. Don't see too many on the road these days."

"Here, hold your arms out," Andree draped him with coats and cleared a space for the new brass lamp.

"Always carting the kids off to one thing or another," he steadied the load with his chin. "It was a very functional automobile."

"A regular shopping machine," she actually jabbed him in the ribs. Loaded back up, we bid Barn guy farewell and headed off into the sunset, the old wagon packed to the gunwales.

"$10,237.66," Andree totaled the receipts. "You really did it this time, buster."

"Get rid of those will ya?"

"Whatever you say, Wilson. First trashcan you see."

"I gotta tell you, the whole time I really felt like I WAS someone else."

"That's funny. I have a sudden craving for someone else," she gave me a wink. "Take me home lover boy."

"Piece of cake. What'd I tell you?"

"I can't believe it's over."

Almost.

"I'd like to cash this."

"Certainly sir, let's see six hundred dollars." The teller ran my check and reached for the cash drawer. I could feel my stomach turning flips.

"Could you excuse me one minute? I'm out of

twenties," she slipped from her stool and headed off to wherever they keep them. When she returned she had a slight, bald headed man with her.

"Mr. Wilson? I wonder if I could have a moment." He nodded me to a nearby desk.

"Is there a problem? I asked.

"Mr. Wilson. It's been brought to my attention that we had a flurry of activity in your checking account over the weekend."

"Is that right?"

"Yes, it appears there were an inordinate number of checks written on that account," he winced. "Forty-seven, to be exact."

"You're kidding."

"No, I'm afraid I'm not kidding."

I edged forward in my chair. "That's a lot of checks."

"It's not the number that troubles us. It's the amounts. The sum total is more than your balance, you see."

"How much more?"

"A great deal more," he nodded in an almost friendly fashion. "We tried to call you, but it seems your phone number is not in service. Naturally we suspected that someone had stolen your checkbook, but... I see you have it with you."

I glanced down at the damn thing clutched in my hand. "So I do."

"Naturally we're concerned," his eyes flicked toward the door. "Of course I'm sure there's a perfectly reasonable explanation."

"Of course," I rose from my chair and tossed the checkbook on his desk. He opened it to the three remaining.

"This is a very serious matter, Mr. Wilson. What

do you intend to do about it?"

Through the window behind him I could see a squad car stuck in traffic.

"Well?" baldy pushed it.

"I'm sorry?"

"These overdrafts. What are you going to do?"

What I always do. Fake left and hit the door running.

SISTER

The elevator doors slide open. The old girls look at us packed shoulder to shoulder and roll their eyes in resignation. More hip to shoulder in my case, beanpole that I am. Andree glances over with a teary smile, make that two beanpoles neck deep in grannies. Add to that they're in costume! The one next to me is a bug of some kind. Her coiled antennae bonk me whenever she turns her head. Directly across is the devil herself, and you know this one really is a devil. Those baby blues brimming with mischief, trouble still, even with the walker. There's a bunny here and Frankenstein there and in back, Darth Vadar in a pink chenille bathrobe.

Best of all, they're nuns every one, with us still though decommissioned, marking the time till they're called to heaven. And while they're waiting... well it IS Halloween.

The doors take forever to close and the ones outside are looking at me, Raggedy Anne smiling coyly, Statue of Liberty with a pink paper torch. She whispers something to the scarecrow beside her and I blush like I always do when the girls talk about me.

We take turns pushing buttons and the doors finally close and either the floors are too far apart or this is the slowest elevator ever. The old girls shout over their deafness, friends and sisters for a lifetime, so right they should finish together.

Muriel introduces us and they ooh and ahh

while we smile and fidget, the two of us eight years old once again, though a decade, at best, from our own dotage.

Then the doors slide open and it's more of the same, a pair of pirates, a coven of witches, cowgirls in wheel chairs ready to roll, a few not quite with it but hanging in there, flapping their gums and scolding their IV bags.

The old nuns, bless 'em.

And we as lapsed as we can be. My last Sunday mass somewhere back in Latin, out of practice but slipping back into it. The nuns will do that to you. A softening of the spirit words can't describe, losing yourself in their good graces, the row house accents, the smell of soap.

The party's just starting when we hit the lobby and it takes a while to push through the crowd. And what a crowd it is! Wrinkled faces smeared in makeup, funny hats and fake moustaches, more Fellini than Fellini, the sort of thing you can't make up.

"The sisters really go all out, eh Muriel?" I guide her out the door.

"I think the full moon has a lot to do with it," she takes my arm.

"Are you sure you want to miss this?"

"Absolutely."

Muriel, aka Sister Pascal, one of Andree's two surviving aunts and as close to a saint as I'm likely to get. Until recently she was a tiny tower of strength, but the years and the hip replacements have taken a toll. She walks like there's a bad connection, which, of course, there is though she's not complaining. Good as new is what she tells us, a real trooper, as Andree's dad would say.

We are here at St. Joseph's to take her to lunch. I

can usually get out of this sort of thing, but Muriel is a favorite of mine and I could use the credit. The truth is I'm a sucker for the old folks. All of them have a story to tell and I'm the one who can pull it out of them. I ask away and Muriel always answers. Andree calls it interrogation but we think of it as banter. In her eyes I see Muriel knows my type well.

We cross the parking lot passed the statue that looks like a logo, our eyes are drawn to the face without features.

"Let me guess. St. Joseph?" I venture.

"So they tell me," Muriel grunts.

"His head looks like a donut."

"It's an abstract. It takes getting used to."

"You hate it, right?"

"It's controversial."

"You hate it."

"Intensely."

She's the matriarch by attrition, from a time when each clan sent a few to the calling. Second oldest of five sisters, Port Richmond born and raised. Just 18 when she joined the convent and I think of her then and I have to wonder. Too young to vote or buy a bottle, old enough to vow it all away. A single photo shows a handsome girl smiling into the sun. A wide brimmed hat, her only extravagance, but quite the extravagance, I must say.

The sister who became a sister, the rest going on to boyfriends then husbands and their share of the baby boom. Like most nuns Muriel became a teacher and like most teachers she worked the circuit, transferred on diocesan whim, Broad Street to Bristol and points in between. Never long enough to become a fixture, at least that's what they must have figured. One of that army of savants and drill sergeants that made

Catholic schools the best in the business. Sixty years at the head of the classroom, past middle age and onto the downside. Those husbands gone, some forgotten, five sister widows left behind. The last years spent in ill health and loneliness. Going, going, and they're gone.

Except for Muriel.

"My problem with St. Joseph is he gets no credit," I say as we turn into traffic. "I mean what was really in it for him?"

"What do you mean 'in it'?"

"Well, he gets to be the husband but not the father, and then after Christmas you never hear of him again."

"Maybe that's the way he wanted it," Muriel smiles.

"But what do we know about him? I mean he's just a footnote."

"We know he was a carpenter."

"Well yeah, OK. He had a job, but the rest they skip over. He doesn't even have any lines!"

"I didn't realize you were a biblical scholar."

"Just basic Catholic school stuff, Sister. I mean was he a good carpenter or just the guy with the hammer."

"He was an excellent carpenter."

"Where does it say that?"

"In the epistles... St. Paul. Corinthians."

"You're making that up," I look to Andree. "She's making that up."

"Do you even own a bible?" Muriel wonders.

"I can get one."

We'd planned on going to the Italian place but when we pull in the lot the sign says Closed. So we drive around arguing scripture until we spot a Beef and Ale with cars in the lot.

"What do you think?" I signal left.

"Tom, it's a bar!" Andree kicks me under the seat.

"Yeah, but they have chicken fried steaks! When was the last time Muriel had a chicken fried steak?"

"What's a chicken fried steak?" Muriel wonders.

"One of the great culinary mysteries," I turn in. "Think of the Trinity without the Holy Ghost."

The place is done up like an English pub. We hang our coats on the booth hook and slide in beneath a fake stained glass window. Out the window is a picture of a deer grazing in a picture of a meadow. The jukebox is playing something by Ella and the barman has a walrus moustache. My kind of place.

"Give us three chicken fried steaks and a round of Guinness," I tell the waitress.

"None for me, thanks," Andree overrules me. "I'll have the garden salad."

I look to Muriel. "Just you and me kiddo,"

"Is it chicken or steak?"

"It's both and it's neither. Trust me on this."

While we're waiting for our order Muriel updates us on the state of the sisterhood, a regular feature of our program and invariably dire. It's not something she'd volunteer on her own, so I make a point to ask. She speaks directly and doesn't flinch.

"So then sister, how are we doing?"

"Not well, I'm afraid. If you can believe it, we're down to four."

"Four nuns?!" Andree bugs her eyes.

"Four enlistees," I set her straight.

"Novitiates," Muriel sets me straight.

"Oh my God, that's awful," Andree tries to conceive of it.

"A widow, a divorcee and two young Guatemalan girls," Muriel breaks it down. "I'm beginning to think we're doomed to extinction."

"Beginning? That biological clock is barely ticking," I ignore Andree's kicks under the table. "What about the average age?"

"It's getting higher."

"Let me guess. The widow and the divorcee are no spring chickens. So that leaves the Guatemalans to hold down the curve. Sheesh! And they'll probably run off with, I don't know, leftist guerrillas or something."

"The numbers are discouraging, but it's the why that concerns me," Muriel says.

"Gee I don't know. Maybe because these days 18-year-old girls have more than two options?" Wise guy that I am.

"That might explain a reduction, but a complete lack of interest?"

"Hey, check the seminaries. They're staying away in droves. But that's another story," which earns me another cautionary kick.

And just what *does* Muriel think of our predator priests? The blackest cloud we could ever imagine, the bad news in bunches that shocks even me, a confirmed infidel and practicing cynic. Muriel can be as candid as I am curious, but neither of us are going there.

"OK, average age then. Gotta be what? Sixty?"

"Sixty-four."

"Jesus, what's the average LIFE expectancy?"

"It's a crisis. What can you do but pray?"

"Well, for one thing they could let the clergy get married. Other religions allow it."

"Perhaps one day," she smiles. "When I'm gone."

"By then it might be academic. I'm just saying if you need more fish you should make the pond bigger."

"Yes. What would be the harm?" Andree shrugs off my clever analogy.

"There's the matter of commitment," Muriel explains, "Celibacy is not a punishment. It's a discipline."

"It's asking too much."

"Yes well," Muriel shrugs. "You know what they say about old dogs."

I study a spotted spoon. "I have an old dog and he's not celibate."

Our food arrives and Andree toys with her salad while Muriel and I dig in. The steaks are superb and we nod and chew as Ella gives way to Dinah. I make a note to remember this place.

"What do you think?" I ask with my mouth full.

"Very good," Muriel nods in earnest. In between bites we throw back the Guinness. The old girl matches me measure for measure. Andree rolls her eyes and spears an olive.

"I suppose they'll be closing schools." I watch Muriel slather a french fry in ketchup.

"Whole parishes, if the cardinal has his way," she pops it in whole.

"And more believers slipping in every day. Can you imagine? A world without Catholic school."

"They can't close them all," Andree hopes against hope. "Where will the mob kids go?"

"That reminds me, Muriel. You ever see any of your old students?"

"Oh my, yes. In fact every Christmas I have dinner with three of them."

"So they made out OK? I mean what do they do for a living?"

She holds my eyes. "They're retired."

"You're kidding." But the math is easy. School kids to pensioners before you know it.

"There's a few more in Brigantine. I see them when we're down the shore."

"They put you up?"

"No, the order has a summer home."

"On the beach?"

"Why yes, we've been going there for years."

Visions of old nuns in bikinis come on before I can stop them, frolicking past until Andree kicks me. I try to recall seeing nuns at the shore, but the nuns in bikinis come popping up again and I excuse myself to grab a smoke. Out in the parking lot the nicotine hits me harder than usual and I feel all fuzzy and I think of the nuns. Catholic school. If you didn't go you have no reference. The stuff of countless novels and comedy routines cannot be known second hand. When I was a kid I envied my public school friends, but the older you get the more you cling to what defines you. Catholic school, which is to say the nuns.

Thirty years later I watch the kids heading off in their uniforms and skinny ties and I know what they face. The rod, the rule, myth and ritual beyond comprehension, truth and faith mixed with wild yarns and glaring gaps of logic. You may not come out of it pure of heart, but you know right from wrong and your handwriting puts the heathens to shame.

What's special in Muriel is easy to see, too sharp to lose advantage and too quick with a laugh not to know how to use it. Every school had one, impish and disarming, passing down from brother to sister. The one who could strike sparks and reach the unreachable. I don't know what Catholic school is like these days, but I'm guessing innocence has taken a hit. Now the pulpit is the last refuge of the scoundrel and the Catholic Church has the scoundrels to prove it. Suffer the children, feed thy lambs, the wages of sin will flatten you.

The sisters taught us that.

"So, why Pascal?" I think to ask as we turn out of the parking lot. "Your official name. How did you decide on it?"

"You are the curious one, aren't you?" Muriel smiles via rear view mirror.

"I've always wondered. It's a great name compared to some. Sister Humphrey Aloysius comes to mind."

Even Muriel wrinkles her nose at that one. Sister Al, my third-grade cross to bear, a name that fit her, warts and all.

"I don't know how the other orders do it, but when you're ready to take your vows they ask you to submit three names for consideration," Muriel tells us.

"Pascal?" I raise a finger. "Isn't he the one that blesses your throat?'

"He is."

"And what a quaint little custom THAT is. Kneeling there with candles crossed at your neck. Scared to death you'll choke on a chicken bone."

"It beats Ash Wednesday," Andree points out.

"He's been known to work miracles," Muriel reminds us.

"I don't know," I check her in the mirror. "I'll take Saint Heimelich every time."

"It's not just choking. Saint Pascal protects against disease."

"That's why you picked him? Or was it the sound. Sister Pascal. From France."

"I didn't pick it."

"What about the three names?"

"They assigned me Pascal. I'll admit it was disappointing at first, but I came to like the sound of it."

"Did any of the others get a name they picked?"

"Not a one," Muriel shakes her head. "But it's funny. A few years ago I was walking around the convent grounds with Sister Margaret Louise and we passed through the cemetery. At the end, just before the gate we saw a grave marked Sister Pascal and behind it, another marked Sister Margaret Louise."

"You're recycled?!?" I yelped.

"Apparently, yes."

An unsettling tradition and clearly deceptive, but it's not like a cool name will get you somewhere. The next Pascal will have a tough act to follow. A namesake with a hundred year legacy, presuming Muriel isn't last in the line. There's a measure of comfort in this strange conveyance. Her tenure may be drawing to a close but a Sister Pascal will be always with us.

The party is down to diehards when we return to St. Joseph's. There's a lone figure singing into a dead microphone while the devil herself bangs out Chopsticks on the piano. There are no lyrics to Chopsticks that I know of, which might account for the dead mike and Sister Satan's devilish grin. Gangs of nuns are gathered at the elevator, gabbing like they haven't seen each other in years. Considering their varying degrees of immobility, it's possible they haven't.

We pile in the elevator and the crowd thins at every floor. Then it's down to us and Muriel's neighbor, Sister Immaculata, a name that never made a wish list. The two go back a long way and I can see the bond and I envy them for it. The years spent in the struggle, a lifetime holding up their end. It's a bond few men live to hope for, weightless as God's grace and stronger than a mother's will. In the end the priests were like our father's, distant and imperious, volatile but avoidable. Like our moms the nuns were entrusted to raise us using wisdom, guile and no more force than necessary. They saw us through the events that shaped us, from A-Bombs to astronauts, presidents to popes.

"You know," Sister Immaculata says to me. "For years people thought Sister Pascal and I were sisters."

"Biological sisters," Muriel explains.

"What do you think?" Immaculata shoulders up. They're both old and both tiny. Any further resemblance would be a stretch.

"Why, it's uncanny," I tell them. "Twin sister sisters."

"Of course, I've put on some weight," Immaculata says, though you'd never know it. The two of them could fit in my pocket.

We visited Muriel's room, an invite I couldn't pass up. The nuns were such a relentless presence it's hard to imagine what they went home to. When we got there I was surprised to see a TV and remote control, an overstuffed chair, an electric coffee maker and yesterday's Inquirer folded on the bed. The room was small, just a cell really, but it's on the top floor and came with a view. Add an ashtray and a beer cooler and it would do me nicely.

"Cable?" I wonder.

"Oh my, yes," Immaculata assures us.

"A gift from Heaven," Muriel concurs.

It's dusk when we bow out with hugs all around and a promise to return. I'm looking forward to keeping that promise. Like most things Catholic St Joseph's has that fade away feel and I can't deny the spirit suits me. We circle the statue and head down the lane, the place lit up like a grand hotel. We pray they'll all meet again in heaven. And if there's a God who holds up his end, he'll see that they're happy forever and ever. Amen.

HUMBOLDT

"Get the gate for me will ya, pardner?"

He's been calling everyone "pardner" for a week now in clear violation of the code. I work the twisted length of wire.

"Other way," he tells me.

"What the hell do we need a gate for anyway?"

"Looks like your finger's bleeding."

I yank the loop off the post. The gate drops on my foot like it always does.

We are on our way to do laundry. We decided on Saturday as laundry day thinking other things would come along to occupy our Sundays through Fridays. This has not been the case. Great gaps of time to kill have reduced us to the mundane, throwing rocks across the river, watching the goats and chickens. Mostly we smoke dope and sleep.

But laundry has gotten away from Steve, which accounts for the duffel bags and his overall appearance. Most Saturdays I launder alone, a practice the locals find as amusing as my daily dip in the icy Matol. In the land of lax hygiene I stick out like a finely groomed thumb.

The thing is, Steve really likes it here. Everyone seems to like it here. I don't know what I was expecting, but counting down to laundry day doesn't ring a bell. I'm all for getting back to the land, just don't get it all over me. For a time I thought that filthy jeans and black socks were Humboldt de rigueur. Then I realized the natives weren't wearing socks.

"Here take this will ya?" Steve hands me one of his bags in exchange for mine, the contents barely rounding the bottom. Past the garden, weed choked and wilting, cultivated in a cocaine frenzy then left to the deer when the Quaaludes came. Skirting the cluster of abandoned trucks and school buses, tiptoeing by the guy who lives in the tree stump, on through the last stand of live oaks and out into open country. A scene as idyllic as Steve swore it would be. Idyllic. The very word taking shape like a row of Greek columns. I can dig it. Skies so blue you lose your balance, grassy hills folding into each other, scattered horses, so right on.

"Oh what a beautiful moooor-ning," Steve's Goulet is right on the money. It's a schtick that gets him stitches only I'm not laughing.

"What's on your mind pard?" he gives me a nudge.

"Pard? What the fuck is pard?"

"Derived from pardner. A rural southwestern colloquialism indicating partnership in, or symbiotic-"

"Give it a break."

"What...? Pard?"

"Or anything derived thereof."

"Whatever you say p-uh-"

Around the bull nose base of Karen's hill, tent flaps open to the breeze, silhouette so still you wonder what she's doing. I worry about Karen, though not enough to keep me from sneaking up there every other night. I fear that she will kill me in my sleep for no reason other than she's bat-shit batty and heavily armed. Maybe part of the attraction, bored shitless and horny as I am. At the crest of the hill we stop to watch a pair of turkey hawks soar on the thermals. We're thinking about what we look like, long-haired and berry brown, eyes all squinty against the sun.

Steve pulls a roach from the cigarette pack in his pocket.

"Rains coming," he cups his hands and fires it up. "I can smell it in the wind."

"Blow me, clown."

Near the flatbed bridge we see dust clouds to the north. A car, or more likely an amalgam of parts cobbled together and bearing makeshift living quarters. These hills abound with vehicular aberrations unseen since the Oakie days. Makes and models unto themselves, as much a part of the White Thorn milieu as baby butts and brown teeth. Breaking out of the far trees in a flash of sunlight, yellow jeep with a dog in back and a real looker at the wheel. The type that strikes a chord of longing, blow dried blonde, and fresh as a daisy, clearly not of this place.

"What have we here?" Steve drops his duffel bag and shades his eyes. A rind of dirt runs from wrist to elbow.

"She must be lost," is all I can think.

"Maybe she came to a fork in the road and just took it."

"Someone should warn her."

"Leave it to me."

The jeep stops at the lip of the bridge. The dog jumps out, circles once then jumps back in when blondie doesn't budge. Sits slouched behind the wheel scanning the hills behind high priced shades.

"Howdy ma'am," Steve gives her his goofiest grin. "What can we do for you this fine morning?"

"Johnny Cash? Is that you?" she rakes her hair straight back so it falls over her face, a move that makes my heart melt.

"The name's Steve. This here's my pardner, Tim," a rare reference to my first name.

"Steve and Tim. How homespun."

"Right purty dog you got there."

She looks to me. "He's kidding, right?"

"He better be," I say, more to him.

She slides sideways out of the jeep and strides over the flatbed, the last few in a slow sashay that's pretty much out of our league. Standing too close as we downright ache for her. Our needy concave faces reflected in her shades, Steve looking less than human in his laundry togs, myself, so much taller and neat as a pin.

"Do me a favor boys, watch Romeo and the jeep while I go buy a horse."

"Give us a ride into town and you got it," I strike the standard deal.

"Sorry, I'm going west. You know, into the sunset?"

"To the road then."

"Play your cards right, cowboy," she turns and heads up the trail, butt cheeks churning for as long as we care to watch. Until she's just a tiny speck veering left and straight up the hill to John's cabin. Not a cabin so much as a carport chained to pine trees and draped in blue plastic, the building material of choice in these parts. Untold acres of it lashed to rooftops and duck taped to shanties, forever not blending in. John of the horses and flamenco guitar, big guy from Yonkers, all I know about John. Watching until we can no longer see her, just the patch of blue where we know her to be.

"Mmmmmmmmmmdoggies!" Steve says before I can stop him.

"Steve... Steven," I step around to face him.

"Lose the gomer routine OK? You're from Pittsburgh. You wouldn't know shitkicker if you stepped in it, remember?"

"Sure thing, Tim," he says in his normal voice.

"'preciate it," to ease the blow.

"I thought I had it down pretty good."

"Too good. It's like hanging out with an imbecile."

"I meant it as an inside joke."

"Too cagey. The cagey starts to fray the nerves."

"For years from now, to get a laugh."

"Also a sort of leering quality to it. Unbecoming."

"But good, though."

"Too cagey. It wasn't working."

"I gotta tell you it feels right. A million miles from home you can be anyone."

"No you can't."

"It's the fu-manchu isn't it?" he gives the ends a twirl.

"No. The fanchu-manchu is another thing entirely"

"Hey Tim, it's 1975. Loosen up a bit."

"One affectation too many, since you brought it up."

We turn our eyes to the hillside. Two figures, one less tiny, move at an angle to the top and over. I picture them coming down the other side, passed the nasty dead thing, over the water line that runs to Karen's, through scrub pines to a small unfenced clearing where John's horses gather for no apparent reason.

"You really want her, don't you Tim?"

"Are you kidding? The first girl I've seen in weeks without head lice?"

"How will you stand it after she's gone?"

"That was my first thought."

"You know what I say don't you?" Steve folds his

arms across his chest.

"What do you say?"

"That's one fine looking woman. Jaysus!"

"I got no problem shooting you, you know."

Steve smiles and slaps me on the back. "Hey! That's more like it, p-uh-."

We gather our bags and start across the flatbed, White Thorn creek a-gurgle below us. The yellow jeep gleams like something perfect.

"I can see it in your eyes, Tim. What you wouldn't give."

"To sleep in clean sheets."

"What we came to get away from."

"Take a shower, watch TV."

"Mere creature comforts, friend. While she's taking a shower and watching TV you're out here living history. Something you can tell your grandkids about."

"Right. The summer I shit behind a tree."

"The last of the badlands. It's crude, I grant you, but so out of touch."

"And the good points?"

Steve shrugs his eyebrows as if the good points are obvious. As if living in a lean-to and shooting smack is a noble rite of passage, as if killing and eating campsite mascots is to be expected, as if helicopter surveillance is a really a good thing.

"When will you ever get a chance to do this again?" he says in all seriousness.

A dozen comebacks come to mind but I hold my tongue. What we're doing, essentially nothing, speaks for itself. Oddly, the moment passes into an interlude so elementally perfect, I swear I can hear the sun shine. The essence of the north coast goes straight to our heads. Stillness, deep and seductive, light and color like no other place, the shadow of a hawk rippling over, the buzz of a fly right out of Steinbeck.

Steve tosses our bags in the back of the jeep and slips in behind the wheel.

"This thing about women and horses," he checks himself in the side mirror. "It's not natural you know."

"Why is that? Men like horses too."

"Not if they don't have to. With women it's genetic."

"Stereotype?" I settle in beside him.

"Exactly. The thing we use to explain away the truth."

"I thought that was reefer."

"Which reminds me," he slips another roach from his pocket, the local blend, ungodly stuff. Here in Humboldt it's not the quantity of drugs, it's the quality. Reefer so potent you can't work a pencil, lines as pure as the driven snow. It's the main reason nothing gets done around here. That and the quantity.

Over Steve's shoulder I see another dust cloud approaching. Tom and Laura's panel truck, by the sound of it, rods knocking as it clears the trees, sheathed in blue plastic and shingled in cedar. Tom's bulbous head lolls behind the wheel, a gaggle of limbs flail in the back, Laura and the triplets, Moe, Larry and Curly. They pull up behind us. Tom grins his half-wit grin and leans on the horn.

"Clampetts at twelve o'clock," I give Steve a nudge. "You better move this thing."

"Me? I haven't driven in months."

"OK, move."

"No wait, I can do it," he reaches for the key then changes his mind.

"Come on, before he comes over here."

"OK," he turns the key and the jeep jumps to life. "Let's see, first gear?"

"Straight up. Just do it, will you?"

He eases the clutch and there's a sudden lurch followed by a thump and a string of blood curdling yelps.

Romeo!

Off like a shot but running funny, the echo of yelps curdling as he lists to the right. Turning to a moan when his front legs crumple, low and mournful like he knows what's coming. Eyes rolled back, tongue flaccid in the dirt, dead before we even get there. The image sears into memory, our end of the deal gone horribly wrong. Confirming what we've always suspected. If there's a way to fuck up we will find it. The dog dead for a minute now, soon to be two and so on. Steve and I kneel on either side, the sun shines, the creek gurgles, but it's all so different now. No way to fix it, over in the blink of an eye. We have done what we came all this way to do.

"Oh Christ, we've killed it."

"Steve, it was an accident.

"Jesus, oh Jesus, what do we do?"

Larry and Curly come up from behind, mouths agape and eyes bulging. Worse yet, a distant scream heads our way.

"Is he dead?" Larry wants to know.

"Did you kill him?" snot-nose Curly, more to the point.

"He's dead all right," Tom says for the record.

"They killed him, OK" Laura sets it straight.

Followed by a crash and splash.

It came out later that Romeo was seven. Prime of life and the picture of health right up to the moment we killed him. If we hadn't, the girl, the dog and possibly a horse may have passed a happy decade together. Of course if we hadn't, Steve might have remembered to set the emergency brake. For Romeo and the yellow jeep, any road not taken could have only been longer.

ACCOMPLICE

Frankie takes the 41 to the end of the line, steps off into a twilight of chirping crickets and fresh cut grass. He walks past Tudor mansions and sprawling haciendas feeling more than a little conspicuous. In the fading light he sees kids on trail bikes circling a cul de sac. A dog barks. A pool filter hums. Dishes clatter in a kitchen sink.

The house at 105 Pennridge Court has a pillared front porch. Whistling a one-note tune Frankie passes by without a glance. He continues on to a grove of trees at the end of the block, picks one with an unobstructed view and shimmies up to a forty-foot perch. A hedge runs along the rear of the house. Lights are on in an upstairs room and a TV flickers through a downstairs window.

Cassie's house reminds Frankie of his grandparents' place in Pennsylvania. He remembers chasing his cousin through piles of raked leaves while his mom and his grandmother battled inside. His mother grew up in a neighborhood like this, a fact that never ceases to amaze him. Once, while searching for her dope stash he stumbled on a shoebox filled with old photographs, Christmas snapshots of Sandy and siblings. He keeps the best one in his wallet, her big eyes and uncertain smile. Already life was proving unmanageable.

Frankie wonders about his mother's latest

transformation—Madame Sandra, Sayer of Sooth. Cassie was her first client and Frankie's favorite, but there are others, long-limbed girls with designer checkbooks. Their cars beam brightly between the gutted wrecks of Beck Street. They huddle with Madame Sandra ignoring Frankie completely. Fact is, his mother has changed in ways miraculous. Bills get paid. Meals are somewhat regular. Actual routines are taking shape. Lately, when he looks in her eyes he sees more than his own reflection. Frankie's hopeful, but at thirteen he knows he's young enough to be fooled.

When it's dark he climbs down from his perch and makes his way to the edge of the woods. The streets are empty. He walks with his head down feeling invisible. At 105 he turns up the drive then veers across the back yard to the hedge. He squats in the bushes recalling his instructions.

"Just take a look around. See what goes on over there," Sandy slipped a dollar bill in his pocket. "Keep out of sight and don't steal anything."

"And if I get caught?"

"Don't get caught, honeybunch. We're talking meal ticket here."

She confides in him now. At first the palms were a problem for her. They looked alike and revealed nothing. But there are easier ways to gauge the fates. An unsolicited trash pickup revealed a preference for imported vodka and ribbed condoms. An intercepted mail delivery spelled out details of a messy divorce and messier settlement. If the future is unforeseeable, the past is as plain as this month's phone bill. In just a few weeks Madame Sandra has learned more about life at 105 Pennridge Court than Cassie knows herself.

Frankie leans his head against the house, feels the TV volume vibrate through the wall. A light clicks on in the window above him. A shadow passes to the snap of elastic. Frankie throws caution to the wind and sneaks a peek. Cassie stands in her underwear making faces in the bathroom mirror. Faces of cold calculation and smoldering desire, faces she will never use. Then a sudden crunch of gravel and headlights sweep over the yard. Frankie ducks and rolls under the hedge, flattening a day-old mound of dog shit. The stench is sudden and stupendous and he buries his face in the dirt to escape it. The car swings around the circular drive stopping less than ten feet away. Two people get out, a man and a woman.

"Whoooeee!" the man fans the air. "Rusty must have just pinched one off."

"Oh, that goddamn dog is ruining my pachysandra," Cassie's mom gripes. They start for the house but the man pauses, so close Frankie could untie his shoes.

"Jesus," he gasps. "Have you checked him for worms lately?"

"It's shit, Roy. Let's not dwell on it."

"Sorry, love. Wouldn't dream of it," he hastens to join her.

As the door swings shut Frankie scrambles to his knees spewing mac and cheese over his shoes. His breath catches in a gag and he whirls in circles pulling at his sweatshirt. Weak and wheezy, icy with sweat, he crawls off trailing pachysandra and coagulating gobs of goo. Inside voices rise and fall, carrying through the siding like voices in a dream, Cassie and her mother having at it. At first Frankie can't make out what they're saying, but when they move to the corner room their words become clear.

"Rodrigo? Who the hell is Rodrigo?" her mother is shouting.

"Come on, mom! I told you. I met him at Tiffany's party. You said I should try and meet new people."

"American people! Jesus, do I have to spell everything out for you?" mother's heels hammer the hardwood. "People named Rodrigo make minimum wage!"

"So that's it! You're a bigot! What about things like equality?"

"Equality is for your hot pants girlfriends baby, not for you."

Their voices fade as they climb the stairs but rise again from the second floor.

"You're ruining my life! I want to go live with daddy."

"That's a laugh. Your father will have your Rodrigo deported."

They rant from room to room, then a door slams and silence stretches. Frankie sits and shivers in the darkness. He wills himself to move but nothing comes of it. The porch door squeaks and Roy steps out, stands at the rail looking up at the night sky. Frankie follows his gaze to a sliver moon, but when he looks back Roy's gone. Frankie strains to hear but no sound comes. His ears pound and his arms and legs stiffen. Roy must have spotted him. He's hiding out there waiting. He's sneaking up with a dagger in his teeth.

Frankie rips through the bushes, hurtles the hedge and clears the driveway in world-class time. Running blind he somehow misses the lawn chairs and glass topped table, the marble birdbath and brick barbecue. Wind whistles in his ears and his feet barely touch the ground. He hits the clothesline chest high like a sprinter hits the tape. A fraction of his life flashes then a million stars explode in his head.

~

The day's first 41 bus hits Pennridge Court at daybreak. Frankie climbs aboard clutching a single dollar bill.

"Got no change, little brother," the driver looks him over.

"Keep it," Frankie struggles to stuff it in the fare box.

"No man, you keep it," the driver grins. "Since you lost the last round I'm gonna let you ride for free. Just sit in back and open a window. The early birds are gonna love you."

Frankie pulls himself along by the handrail. The motion makes him dizzy and the lights hurt his eyes. He sticks his head out the window but it doesn't help. Slouching low he lifts his shirt to a braided welt embossed in clothespins.

"OH MY GOD, WHAT HAVE THEY DONE TO YOU?" Madame Sandra's voice screeches like a worn set of brakes. Frankie staggers through the kitchen and collapses on the living room sofa.

"OH MY GOD, NOT ON MY SOFA!" Her cries rip across his brain. Contusions and abrasions vie for his attention. His clothes are crusted in filth and his head looks curiously lopsided. He feels worse than he looks.

"WHAT HAVE THEY DONE TO YOU? HOW DID THIS HAPPEN?" Madame Sandra flies around the room raining cigarette ashes over the rug. He tries to track her movements but his eyes refuse to rotate.

"It's OK, mom," he croaks. "No one saw me."

"NO ONE SAW YOU? I SUPPOSE YOU DID THIS TO YOURSELF?"

"It's OK," he tells her again. "It's OK," he can say it without moving his lips.

"Tell me what happened. Did you find out

anything?" Madame Sandra pulls up a chair and sits facing him. "Cassie called last night. She was upset but she wouldn't say why. She'll be over this afternoon and I need something to tell her."

"Rodrigo," he whispers.

"What...? Rodrigo?" she leans over and shakes his leg. "Hey, talk to me. Who is Rodrigo?"

"Cassie... boyfriend... big fight with mom," Frankie's lips stick together with every "b".

"This Rodrigo, where did she meet him? Do you know?... FRANKIE!" she pounds his leg with her fist.

"Party... Tiffany..." he lets his head fall back. Something pops in his neck as his eyeballs settle painfully in their sockets.

"THAT'S IT? A BEANER BOYFRIEND? Oh baby, that's fantastic!" She claps her hands and a thousand bazookas explode in his head. Madame Sandra rushes off and he hears her crooning on the telephone. Frankie stares up at the ceiling. The neon palm buzzes in the window.

THE LIP

When Julie left she took half their stuff. Leo found a checklist and a note under her key ring on the counter. Even with Mario's help it must have taken most of the day. The note said she was leaving the car. He could make the payments or sell it, Julie's way of being more than fair. There were several points he would have contested, but Leo had to admit she'd been generous. All his wives had been generous. It was small consolation.

For days afterward Leo's life was like a dream. He thought about Julie and Mario driving across the country. In his head they were always whooping it up. He wished them dead in the desert, their bodies black and bloated. The image so disturbed him he wished them back to life.

To take his mind off things Leo went to the ball game. He brought his binoculars, a bag of salted peanuts, two joints and his Walkman. The right-hander Rivera was going for the Phillies, big kid, clueless. Leo sat in one of the empty sections under the scoreboard. The binoculars gave him a bird's eye view of the strike zone. From the first pitch Leo could tell the kid had it. Every fastball punched a dust-cloud from the catcher's mitt just before the clap of leather reached him in center field. The big lug got hammered early, but for two and a half hours Leo didn't think of Julie once.

The following Sunday he drove to Rittenhouse Square and read the paper. The park was crowded but no one approached him. Julie would be in San Francisco by now, badmouthing him to their west coast friends. Funny, none of them had called. He pictured the other half of their stuff in a North Beach apartment, sun streaming in the windows, Chronicle spread over the sofa. He could see it clearly.

That night Mario called. Julie had dumped him as soon as they hit the city.

"Swear to God, Leo, I never laid a hand on her," he insisted.

"What are you calling me for?"

"Hey man, I feel like a shit."

"You are a shit."

"I'm coming back, Leo. You can kill me if you want to but I can't take it here."

"Come on back. I won't kill you."

"Oh man, I feel like such a shit."

Mario showed up on Friday. Despite his rejection he looked much the same, half-drunk, pacing the kitchen berating himself.

"I mean how could I do that to you?" he jabbed a finger in his own chest. "My best fucking friend! What the fuck is wrong with me?"

"You're a shit. You couldn't help it."

"You're right, Leo. You've always said it but now I believe it."

"Believe it."

He stayed three days then left to mooch off a cousin. Mario was related to half the wops in South Philly. Leo had never known him to have a place of his own. What did he expect to do in California?

On Easter Sunday Leo walked to his mother's. As always, he was taken by the photos on the walls, chronologically arranged portraits, Leo and his sister

Gail, Gail and her two kids, one of his dad in a straw hat over the mantel. Gail divorced and moved to Florida two years ago leaving Leo to deal with the obligations. The tone never varied.

"I don't understand my own children," his mother slipped a Camel from the pack on the table. "Your father and I were married forty-five years!"

"Thirty-five, mom. Dad died ten years ago," Leo reminded her.

"You should have grabbed Mrs. Ruggerio's Eileen. She was always crazy about you."

"No moustaches ma. It's where I draw the line."

She tilted her head back to work the bifocals "Oh sure, the neighborhood girls weren't good enough for you."

He let her go on, wondering what it would be like when she died. He'd returned to Philly after her last stroke, determined to see her through to the end. Six years now and she never looked better.

"Your father was right," she handed him a beer from her little cooler. "You're a bungler, Leo. You could have joined the business, but no. You had to go to California. You had to marry every floozie who came down the pike. And to think we almost gave you up for adoption."

Leo slid in beside her on the sofa. "You're right, mom. I should have been a salesman. I should have married Eileen Ruggerio, but," he held up a finger, "at least I didn't murder my mother, like Richie Pettis."

"Richie was a bastard, but he was no bungler," she gave him a poke. "Besides, who was it that sent your father to an early grave, aanh?"

"... He had emphysema, for Christ sake!"

"You know what I mean." The bifocals gave her a haughty look. Leo *didn't* know what she meant but he let it pass. The smoke from her cigarette curled into a perfect circle. He never came without a carton, hoping against hope.

They ate microwaved chicken, raw on the inside. Leo could hear the clack of dentures over the talk show radio. Afterwards he did the dishes and put out the trash. Standing in her tiny yard he raised his eyes to the South Philly skies. One star, way over Jersey.

"Star light, star bright, first star I see tonight," he tried to remember the rest. The light circled slowly and descended to the airport. When he returned his mother was sound asleep in front of the TV. He leaned to kiss her forehead, slipped a twenty from her purse and let himself out.

There was a postcard from Julie in the morning mail. "I love you but I don't like you."

Benny was waiting for him at the diner. The Sheik, Julie called him in reference to the doo, jet black and raked back like it was painted on. Not a good look for Benny, nearing sixty and putting on the pounds.

"Where you been?" he hiked his eyebrows. "I'm on a schedule here."

"What schedule?" Leo checked the clock. "The tit bars don't open for hours."

"Yeah, OK, that's funny. Sit down, would you? I got a kink," Benny rubbed his neck.

"Maybe you should give the girls a break for a while. Everything in moderation, eh Sheik?"

"Yeah, that's funny."

"Not that it's pathetic or anything."

"I just thank God I lived to see the day. You only go around once, kid. Tell me a better way to spend the time?"

Leo smiled. "Well, it's good you found your niche."

"Tell me you got HD, Leo."

"What I got is ceiling fans. Top of the line and in the box."

Benny's eyebrows shot up higher. Everything was eyebrows with the Sheik.

"What the fuck am I gonna do with ceiling fans? What about the TVs?"

Leo tapped his pudgy little hand. "Next time, Benj. This time it's ceiling fans."

"Jesus, Leo. Tell me it ain't down to this."

"It's down to this, Benny," Leo flapped his hands around. "Hey it beats scalping tickets, right?"

The Sheik sat there staring off. "I don't know what happened. What the fuck happened?"

"Prosperity, Benny," Leo shrugged. "It's a socio-economic thing."

"Jesus, I miss the old days. This..." he shook his lacquered head.

"Benny, hey, these are top of the line fans here. You want in?"

He just kept shaking his head.

"Tell you what," Leo drummed his thumbs on the counter. "Give me two grand for the whole load. That's one hundred units, plus remote."

"Units. God help us."

"I can deliver them or you can come pick them up. Your call."

The Sheik heaved a sigh and reached in his jacket. Leo waited but the hand just stayed there.

"Look at you," the old crook laughed. "Hey this reminds me of the scene in that movie where the guy reaches for his wallet and pulls out his gun."

"What movie? What are you talking about,

Benny?"

"The movie where the hoods hijack a truckload of something, not ceiling fans. I forget."

"In or out, c'mon Benny."

"Coffins, that's what it was," Benny leaned in close. "Only some of them was occupied."

"Time's up." Leo stormed off, slowing slightly to give Benny an opening. When the bastard declined he pushed through the door and crossed the lot to the black SUV. He felt out of focus, not all there, a flash to the 80's with his head full of Tester's. Not like Benny to queer a deal. Sheik could move broken glass and at the lowball price he had to know Leo was desperate. What was it with the old guys that they got so goofy? The problem was who else can you go to?

The other problem was what to do with them now? The ceiling fans. They were in Ludlow's garage at the moment, but his wife was squawking and his neighbors were nosey. Not to mention Leo's sudden cash flow problem.

He watched Benny through the window, willing him to change his mind. For a second he thought it just might work, but the fat fuck sat there feeding his face.

A Julie message on the machine.

"I think you should resolve your conflict with your mother. She won't be around much longer, you know. "

Leo wondered who she could be staying with and drew up a list of likely suspects. The thing that always bothered him, he could picture Julie with almost anyone. She came late to the cheating game, but it didn't take her long to get the hang of it. Catholic schoolgirl turning with a vengeance. He played the message a second time. The phone rang while he was looking at it.

"Leo?"

"Yeah Luds. I'm gonna move 'em, don't rip a stitch."

"That's what I called about. They're not here."

"What?"

"The ceiling fans. I came home tonight and they were gone,"

Leo pictured Ludlow's garage, the space they took up.

"I know you'll think I'm getting over but someone stole them, Leo. I swear to fucking God."

"Someone walked off with a truckload of ceiling fans?"

"Fucking un-believable, right?"

Lying rat-fuck son of a bitch.

"You don't want to do this, Ludlow. Couple of days, they'll pop up, right?"

"On my father's fucking grave, Leo. Hey, I'm out just like you!"

Leo thought he heard someone else talking, but he couldn't be sure. He didn't want to think about what was happening here. Ludlow meant to beat him on the load.

"Couple of days. Ludsy. I'll give you a call."

The Phillies were in a rebuilding year. Except for one championship season, that shining moment decades past, the Phils had been rebuilding for over a century. Once again pitching was the problem. Pitching was always the Phillies problem, except for the odd year when hitting was also the problem. Many like Leo saw the organization as genetically flawed, those fluke years in the 80's, just a statistical anomaly. Throw the monkeys out on the diamond often enough etc.

Only not THESE monkeys. Their record was

more than a matter of bad judgment. Touted prospects shed their talent as they moved through the system. High school phenoms left their confidence and their fastballs in Spartansburg and Wilkes-Barre. Management, depending on the year and level of hostility, made one of two wrong moves. Either they let this year's wunderkind languish in the bush leagues, tying up time and money, or they rushed him into the rotation where he was promptly battered beyond recognition. Pick a year, same story.

Tonight's pitcher was a recent pickup from Houston. Front office couldn't resist these guys, the one season whiz with a flakey reputation, career castoffs cycling down. All too often it ended with the Phillies.

The first pitch was a strike, triggering visions of a strikeout. The season was young and hope springs eternal. The second pitch was strike two swinging and even the cynics allowed themselves to dream. Pitches three, four and five sailed up, up, and away and the rustle in the stands set the seasonal tone. After a confab with the catcher the castoff bore down, fucking beachball coming at ya. Leo could see the batter's eyes light up then a white blur slicing down the right field line. The game quickly settled into a rout, brutal even by Phillie standards. The fans turned ugly early, taunting the castoff with death threats, burying him in boos when they yanked him in the second. Stunned by their rage he stumbled off the field, disappearing into a dugout from which he would never again emerge.

A parade of relievers was promptly pounded.

By the seventh the crowd sat in grim silence, reflecting on all things Philadelphian. Leo was aware of a disturbing parallel between the team's fortunes and his own. It was no coincidence that he spent the glory year in California, watching on TV. The implications were clear and Leo had vowed never to go home again. If that was the price he was willing to pay it. Julie, of course, had other ideas, his mom had her stroke and the rest was just history repeating itself. Of the teams who excelled at futility, none could touch those Fumblin' Phils. Losers of more games than any team in any sport... ever!

They were new and splashy, but they were still row houses. Two where three used to be, bay windows facing out on the drycleaners. Leo parked behind a row of pickups and listened for Lanny's blather.

"What the fuck is this? I got fucking monkeys working for me!"

Rear bedroom, upstairs. The front door was open, the downstairs rooms were bland and tasteless. Leo's own house had the original woodwork, circa 1917. He'd bought it for a song before he met Julie. The thing about modern is it lacked the detail. He waited for windbag to take a breath, but Lanny was on an ass-chewing roll.

"Look at this! There's more fucking paint on the carpet than there is on the fucking wall!"

Leo watched from the doorway. A trio of Mexicans shrugged it all off.

"Nice ceiling fans," he called over.

"Heyyy! Leo my man!" Lanny broke it off and clapped him on the shoulder. "Whaddya think? Federal Terrace, my piece de resistance!"

"Where'd you get 'em Lanny?"

The big man took his arm and led him to the hallway "Yo Leo, you workin' for L and I, or what?"

Leo hated this shit. "Tell me now while I'm still in a good mood."

Lanny looked more puzzled than worried. "Some

guy came around. I didn't ask questions."

"Know something, boss?" Leo pointed with his chin. "Those amigos can't understand a thing you're saying."

Lanny looked in on the Mexicans and smiled. "Best fucking crew I ever had. They'd paint each other if I gave them the word."

"Tell me about this other guy. Do I know him?"

"I wasn't around. Maybe Pedro here can–"

"Cut the crap, Irish."

Lanny looked right through him. "I gotta tell you man, the tough stuff doesn't suit you."

He really hated this. Ludlow was making some kind of move and betting Leo would roll over. Ceiling fans, for Christ sake!

"I got nothin' to do with this," Lanny stood his ground. "Hey, I'm just trying to make a living."

Leo left a footprint on the front door

This was serious. Ludlow had always been flakey, but they'd been at this for thirty years! Leo called and got the machine. He drove over but no one answered the door. After that he didn't know what to do. Ludlow tended bar on the Ave. The place was a dive, mostly ironworkers and off-duty cops. Not a place to start something, but what did Leo plan to start, anyway?

He went to McGrath's to think it through, but they had the game on and Shank was there and the night got away from him. Next morning he spotted Ludlow's truck in the diner lot. Leo signaled to turn but changed his mind, nearly clipping a roofing truck.

Julie on the machine again. Leo didn't even play it.

"Whaddya mean whaddya do? You go after him!" Mario made a chopping motion. "You make him fucking *pay!*"

Leo stared at his hands. "I've known Ludlow all my life."

Mario stumbled to a chair, winded. "Everybody's known him all their lives. What's that got to do with it?"

"I don't want to hurt him."

"He's a piece of shit!"

"I don't have the time for this."

Mario gave him a poke. "That's what he's counting on, dude. You blow it off, you're out of business."

Leo looked at him. "What business? I'm peddling ceiling fans and eating at my mother's!"

Mario plopped his hands on the armrests. "I'm just saying, you take it from Luds, you take it from everyone. It's a business liability."

"He's a brick shithouse!"

"So you pay somebody.... Yo pal," he bent into Leo' line of vision. "This is pretty basic stuff."

He tried the number for the hundredth time. Ludlow answered on the fifteenth ring.

"Yeah what?"

"It's me, Leo."

Silence.

"We gotta talk, Luds."

"We got nothing to talk about. I told you, Leo, the fans were boosted."

Leo looked to Mario. Mario looked away.

"Mario says I should come after you." Leo ducked an empty beer can.

"Mario? That fucking lowlife?"

"But I say we can work this out. Like gentlemen, whaddya think, Luds?"

"Tell Mario to go fuck himself."

"I get my half and I forget all about it," Leo talked the talk.

"Come on, Lip, what are you gonna do? I say they

were boosted they were boosted. You can think whatever Mario wants you to."

"Don't do this, Ludsy."

"Gotta go."

A rainout forced a double header. Leo sat away from the crowd. He watched the game and thought about Luds and how he should have seen this coming. Ludlow was a crook. And Mario was right, once word got out all accounts would go into arrears. Leo couldn't take a hit right now. He was living on credit cards as it was.

The Phils scored in the first. He thought of dropping a dime on Luds then ruled it out. Then the cops are in and everyone's pissed and he's out of business anyway. Should have gone to college with the rest of the goobers. Should have joined the fucking business. Had to be a hustler, no nine to five for Leo the Lip. Now Ludlow wanted to muscle in. Who muscles in on ceiling fans?

Pittsburgh scored three in the fifth and the Phils yanked the starter. Leo spotted Pete Newlin but pretended not to. Predictably, Pete failed to pick up on it.

"HEY LEO! HEY, RIGHT HERE!" he waved his arms and started over.

"Hey Newlin, I'm kinda busy right now."

"I just wanted to tell you, that Jackie Ludlow is an asshole."

"Thanks."

"I told Dooley and them. I said you'd beat the balls off him."

"Again, thanks."

"That fucker will rue the fucking day, yo!"

Pittsburgh scored three more in the eighth. Leo didn't stick around for game two.

~

Luds' truck was in the driveway. Leo circled the block a few times then parked in the church lot.

"OK, Now what?" he asked himself.

Butch Isler had called offering his services. Not out of loyalty, Ludlow just pissed people off. Leo said he'd get back to him but he knew he wouldn't. Even if he wanted to, he couldn't afford it. Big Butchie was top of the line.

By now the news was all over Pennsport. The early line gave Leo the nod with an assist to Butchie. Every passing minute made it worse. If the other shoe didn't fall soon he wouldn't be able to show his face.

And Ludlow *was* crazy. Once Leo made a move it would be his turn and it wasn't hard to guess where the money would go on that. Which left what?

Dory answered the door, walked him to the yard like she didn't have a clue. Who was she kidding? Ludlow sat at the picnic table talking on the phone. He saw Leo in the doorway and rolled his eyes.

"Yeah, I know, that's why I'm calling," he growled into the phone. "You're damn right I'm pissed. Now how do you want to do it?"

Leo sat opposite. Ludlow yacked and yacked. Leo reached over and pressed the button.

"Hey Leo, what the fuck?"

"Sit down, Luds. Your neighbors are gawking."

"Fuck them and fuck you too."

"What are you gonna do, hump around to every job site in the city?"

Ludlow smirked. "Face it, Leo, you've lost the touch. You let that old dago, Benny jerk you around for nickels on the dollar. I get forty a pop for 'em."

"OK, I see your point. Give me my grand and go peddle your wares."

"Or else what?"

Leo watched a small bird hop across the driveway. He thought of Julie lying in the sun on Goat Rock Beach. He got up from the table and shoved his hands in his pockets.

"Yo Luds. That's it?"

"Hey, we can go around and around but basically... yeah."

Leo left by the side gate. He could hear the big fuck laughing on the phone as he crossed the street. In his head he saw himself go to the car and get his gun. One to the chest, one to the head was how you fixed these things. Only Leo didn't have a gun. The only time he ever *shot* a gun was on the boardwalk in Wildwood. Plus, if he killed Ludlow he'd have to go to prison. No fucking way he was going to prison over ceiling fans.

Still he thought about it.

On the way home he passed Zero and Lou on the Quarthouse corner. They fell all over themselves pretending not to see him.

In the morning Leo woke with a rock in his gut. He wondered about the way it was here, the deep end as the standard course of action. It wasn't normal, it couldn't be. This was as close to murder as Leo would get, but he knew it wasn't all that close. He could handle himself in a spot, but he didn't have a murder in him. He knew it and Ludlow knew he knew it.

If there was a way out Leo couldn't find it.

"So I've been thinking..." Julie paused.

"OK."

"We could try it again, Leo. I know now that I need you."

"To what? Help you move?"

"OK, I deserve that. I know I was a shit about

Mario, but he's so..."

"You gotta stop calling Julie. Please."

"You miss me, Leo. Marianne told me you hardly ever come out of the house."

Leo unplugged the phone. The next day he sold the SUV.

"Leo, hey! Jesus Christ! What's it been, ten years?"

"How are you Len? You look good."

"Hey! I heard you got married a while back. How's it working out?"

"It didn't," Leo shrugged. "I make a lousy husband."

"Tell me about it. I get a different set of kids every freaking weekend."

Leo took the chair across the desk. "I see your mug in the papers, real estate broker extraordinaire. You've done well, Len."

He gave his paunch a pat. "Well, I can't complain. But you didn't come all the way down here to sing my praises. What is it I can do for you, Leo?"

"I want to sell."

Len looked offended. "Your place? It's a jewel box, man. I can't let you do it!"

"Got to. I owe some money. Plus I think my ex has her eye on a slice."

"Well, she'll get that, friend. Community property."

"Maybe not. It's still in my name."

Lenny's gaze dropped to his shoes. "Jeez, I don't know, Leo. It sounds unethical."

Leo pulled a wad from his pocket and slapped it on the desk. "One thousand up front. Plus five percent."

Len didn't even look at the money. "Maybe we can finagle something."

"It's gotta be fast. All offers considered, I'll take the hit. And I'd like it to be someone, you know... responsible."

"I have that someone in mind as we speak."

"And no sign. It's gotta be discrete."

"I think I can handle this for you without much problem, Leo."

"Like I said. Extraordinaire."

Leo walked away with 150 thou. Not bad for the old neighborhood, bless the Irish and their woodwork. He left a message on Gail's machine and stashed 50 grand in his mother's account. He'd send an address when he turned up. Palm Beach, maybe, hustle the widows. Or Tempe. He heard it was nice in Tempe.

THE NEIGHBORS

My mother is standing on a bench in the spare bedroom. I can see by the certainty of her movements that she's done this before.

"Look," she points. "They turned the refrigerators around. Sanders must have told them I complained."

Through the window I can see two rusting refrigerators standing flush against the back of the neighbor's house. The refrigerators are just two of the many things that bother my mother about the neighbors. They are loud and profane, throwbacks to the hillbillies who settled along the river in pre-suburban days. Some of my childhood friends came from such families, although my mother doesn't know this. She thinks my friends were from neighboring developments.

There's a mountain of aluminum siding in their backyard. They put their garbage out for collection only when the plastic bags threaten to engulf the house. My mother refers to the siding as "refuse" and she's got a point. It's mostly broken pieces, too short to be of any use. From her perch on the bench she can see all of it: the siding, the bags, the wire frame of the mattress they burned two summers ago. I can see only the refrigerators, but I know what the rest looks like. If I were any kind of son I'd have it out with them.

My mother moved here fifteen years ago, twenty years after the death of my father. At 68, she's been a widow most of her life. My father died when he was four years younger than I am now. My image of him has never faded, big and angry. If he were here the neighbors would not be a problem.

I have two brothers and two sisters. We're not what you would call close, although I have heard from my sisters lately—about the neighbors. My brother Ray has a problem with alcohol, so I don't see him much. The family gathers at my mother's house for Christmas every year with our ever changing cast of spouses and children. We arrive in our late model cars and trudge to the back door, ignoring the mess next door. My father wouldn't recognize us.

What happens with Ray is he goes crazy when he drinks. Certifiable. One time he left his house in a drunken rage and plowed his car into a pole. He hadn't gone far, so he walked home, got his girlfriend's car and plowed that one into a different pole. You can't hurt him when he's in this state, but he can destroy everything. Each year when the Christmas gathering is breaking up, I want to take my brother to the nearest bar, get him plastered, then turn him loose on the neighbors.

I watch my mother move from the bench to the bed, standing on her tiptoes to peer over the curtain. She's a spry 68. Since moving here she's put on weight. It makes her look shorter, though she may, in fact, be shorter. Her boys are tall like their father, but thin like she used to be. When she hugs me, which is often, her head fits right under my chin. It's been that way since I was fourteen

"It's just not right," she mutters. "At first I thought they would go away. People like that are usually so unstable. Sometimes I think they stay just to spite me."

"Mom, come down from there before you hurt yourself."

She turns to me, and slaps her hands against her sides.

"Look at me. I never thought I'd be like this."

When I was nine years old, I came down with St. Vitus Dance. Not for me those conventional diseases. I don't know how St. Vitus figured into it, but the dance part was accurate enough. The virus attacks the nervous system and is characterized by sporadic twitching. It's a painless but serious disease. My mother has since convinced me that my life was on the line. When I was sick she convinced me to get better. When you're a kid, sometimes that's all it takes.

The summer I had St Vitus Dance she bought me a radio for my birthday. When I think of that radio I realize how old we're getting to be. It was brown plastic with rounded shoulders and a grille like a Buick. The tuner knob was in the center of the grille and when you turned it a needle moved across an orange band. They haven't made radios like that in forty years. At night I could pick up stations from other cities, faraway ball games and radio serials. I would lie in my bed with my ear to the speaker, turning the knob in the smallest increments. By summer's end I'd developed the touch of a safe cracker.

One night I listened to a woman in Fort Wayne, Indiana, describe how she shot a man who tried to break into her house. I can remember picturing a man in a suit and hat climbing through an open window. I don't know why, but I've never forgotten that.

"I don't have to put up with it! I simply don't!" my mother declares.

~

She made a lifelong commitment never to be a burden on her children, but until fairly recently my mother was young herself. She lives alone. Last summer the neighbors had someone living in a tent in the backyard. She complained to the police and they made them take it down. Two days later her leaf blower was stolen from the garage. I wanted to go over and confront them, but she forbade it. She knows that when I leave she will be alone. I do count on that.

By contracting, then surviving an exotic disease, I became my mother's favorite. My brothers and sisters never held it against me. St. Vitus Dance impressed even them. For years I had to take penicillin pills and there was always a container in the refrigerator to remind them of my precarious hold on life. The doctors confirmed I might have died, but I suspect doctors often say that when someone pulls through.

When I was well enough to get around, I used to crawl out on the roof at night with my radio and listen to ball games. I'd developed such a deft touch with the tuning knob that I could pick up the Cardinals, the Pirates, Detroit, the Yankees, and the Mets. I would lie on my back on the warm roof shingles and stare up at the stars, imagining my radio pulling signals out of the sky. Those are my fondest childhood memories.

"It's Sanders' fault. Why doesn't he fine them?" my mother wants to know.

I wish I could tell her. Sanders is the police chief. His interest in the case has waned. I have written several strongly worded letters to Sanders on my mother's behalf. He has chosen not to reply. I have made sporadic phone calls to the police station, but he's never there. For this I am grateful, it shames me to say. I am not good at this sort of thing. Since I spent a decade in California shirking family responsibility, my brothers and sisters have assigned this to me. In two weeks I am to appear before the local board of supervisors to plead my mother's case. The idea terrifies me. In the meantime my mother is slowly losing her grip. She is obsessed with the neighbors and the police chief. She speaks of nothing else. She keeps a journal of all the violations, including photographs. I find slips of paper with surveillance notes and inspirational messages to herself. It's like a bad TV movie. A psychological thriller.

As my mother's favorite I was encouraged to be artistic—another pursuit for which I am ill suited. I thought of myself as a writer, but the ensuing years have proven otherwise. There is no work in progress, no novel or collection of short stories to support the illusion. I once wrote a letter to a newspaper columnist who thought enough of it to paraphrase it in his column. This is the extent of my literary recognition. I kept it taped to my refrigerator until it turned yellow.

"Oh, if your father were only here to see this," my mother laments.
"You should move, mom."
"Never!"

I've tried thinking of ways to distract her from this obsession. For a while I talked of returning to California, but she didn't take it seriously. I pretended to be working on a novel and even plagiarized a chapter to pique her interest, but she couldn't be budged. I even considered faking a St. Vitus Dance relapse. The symptoms are easy enough to mimic, but something told me not to. I'd planned on a longer visit, but two hours of this is all I can take.

I check all the doors and windows before I leave.

For the next week I think about my mother constantly. I am obsessed with her obsession. I suspect a real man would take the matter in hand and force a resolution. I've noticed that lately the news is filled with stories of neighborhood disputes that flare into violence. I'm not a violent person, but I've never considered myself a coward. I must admit to sparks of exhilaration in all this. I can't stop wondering what will happen.

My brother Frank calls about "the problem". He lets me ramble on about the board of supervisors meeting and my latest attempts to contact Sanders, but I can sense his dissatisfaction. He tells me to keep him posted. His tone suggests that other options are being considered. Frank is a partner in an engineering firm—a man who has come to expect results.

There's a message on my machine when I get home from work. My mother. The neighbors have added a boat to their collection of debris. I agonize for an hour before calling the police. To my horror the chief answers on the first ring.

"Sanders here."

"Uh, chief, this is Joe Fenner. Listen, I'm calling about my mother. It seems the neighbors have parked a boat in their yard."

"Little sailboat. Picked it up yesterday afternoon."

"You know about it?"

"Sure do. I had to help them with the trailer hitch."

"But chief, they can't keep a boat in their yard."

"Just till summer. They're taking it down the Chesapeake."

"But that could be months from–"

"You tell your mom they'll have that boat out of there by the first of June. They just have to paint it and plug the holes. June first, tell her. Maybe sooner."

"But chief–"

"Listen, I got a call here. I'll get back to you."

"Yeah, OK."

One night when I was up on the roof I heard my parents arguing in their bedroom. My mother's words were muffled, but I could hear my dad loud and clear. He was talking about sending me to a military academy. It would be good for me, he insisted. It would get me headed in the right direction and teach me discipline. My father was a firm believer in discipline. He claimed that the new friends I would make would help me in the future. He said my old friends would never amount to anything and, in fact, they never did.

I crawled to the peak of the roof and poked my head over the edge. The light from the bedroom window cast a faint square on the grass and I could see my father's shadow pass through it as he paced the room. He was trying to sell her on the idea. I could picture him prying his fingers from his fist as he listed the benefits. Teach me independence, teamwork, discipline, always discipline. From his tone I knew that my mother was resisting. I prayed for her to spare her favored son.

They sent brother Ray instead.

Clearly my efforts to deal with the problem are doomed to fail. My pending confrontation with the board of supervisors will resolve nothing. Any action taken against the neighbors will expose my mother to retaliation and that, too, will be my problem. The situation is beginning to take a toll. I'm unable to sleep at night and my work is beginning to suffer. I wince when the telephone rings. My mother leaves long, rambling messages and I worry she's been drinking. My siblings leave messages voicing their concern.

I am driving to my mother's when it hits me, a germ of a solution. What's to be done with these people, these slovenly neighbors who prey on helpless old mothers and their helpless sons? Quite simply, nothing. In the unlikely event that my meeting with the board results in some action, the neighbors will still be there. And as long as they're there they will drive my mother crazy. She must be made to see that moving is the only way out. Desperate measures are called for and a desperate measure is just what I have in mind.

She is in the backyard taking pictures of the boat when I get there. I lead her into the house and recount my conversation with Sanders. She doesn't take it well. I force myself to listen as she rants and raves. Sanders and the neighbors are "in cahoots" she maintains. It is strange to hear her use such a word. Instead of reasoning with her I encourage her outrage, inferring that the board of supervisors and zoning committee are in "cahoots" as well. They view her complaint as a nuisance, I say. All involved are determined to drive her from her home.

When she is sufficiently agitated I take her by the hand and sit her down in the living room.

"There's only one thing left to do, mom."

She looks at me hopefully.

"We'll have to kill them."

Once, during my artistic period I wrote a story about a man who hires someone to kill his wife. It wasn't a good story, but it made me think about how to go about it. Now, as I sit in my mother's living room, watching her face run the emotional gamut, I level my gaze and arch an eyebrow.

"I know a guy," is all I say.

"My God, you're serious. Do you realize what you're saying?"

"It's got to stop. Don't worry, mom I'll handle everything."

"Oh Jesus, what have I done?" she buries her head in her hands.

This is just the reaction I was counting on. If I can convince her I'm crazy enough to consider murder, she will forget about the neighbors and worry about me instead, the favorite, just like old times.

"OK, just the old man." I pretend that it's the sheer number of people to be killed that's putting her off. She shakes her head and sobs.

"This guy knows what he's doing, mom. I promise you, it will look like an accident."

"STOP!" My mother clamps her hands over her ears.

I kneel beside her and take her hand. I'm pulling out all the stops now.

"Look, I know this is hard for you," I kiss her wedding band. "You don't have to worry. I'll make all the arrangements."

"Please, don't talk like that."

I give her hand a squeeze. "Remember when I was sick and you promised me I'd get better? I knew you'd take care of me. Now it's my turn to take care of you."

"I didn't mean for this to happen. I'm so sorry," she sobs and all my anxieties melt away. She will move now. Whatever she thinks of the neighbors, it's not worth a son's madness. We'll find a nice place for her near my sister and then we can all get on with our lives.

"Tell me you didn't mean that, Joey," she sniffles. "Tell me you were just making a joke."

"You're my mother," I force a tear. "They can't push you around. I won't let them."

"Sit down, Joey."

I love this. She hasn't called me Joey in years.

"When your dad died I just wanted to crawl into a hole. I had five kids and no prospect for a future. But I had to be strong. I had to struggle to make a life for you kids, to see you got raised properly. When you were all grown I just wanted to retire to my little house and grow old gracefully. This is my little house. Those are my neighbors. But it's just another problem, honey. I've had problems all my life. Sooner or later they'll move or I'll move and it will all be forgotten. To think that I could drive you to think of such a thing makes me realize how selfish I've been about this. It makes me sick."

"But mom–"

"No, Joey. I don't want to hear anymore."

I drive home feeling better than I have in years. Not only have I neutralized the dreaded neighbors, I've rekindled my mother's maternal instincts. She will be mom again, peppy and independent. Hell, I've probably added years to her life. I sing along with the radio imagining calls of congratulations from my brothers and sisters.

There's a message on my machine when I get home. It's my mother.

"This man you know... is he reliable?"

WELL CONNECTED

Debby leans into the TV light and I see the screen reflected in her glasses. We are surfing the news channels trying to get more info on the murder one trailer park over, a stabbing in broad daylight. Some guy answered the door and got carved up pretty good.

"You'll see, it's a ruse," Deb rearranges the cat on her lap. "Cops make it sound like a random thing, a maniac to cover their ass. Give it two days and they'll change their tune."

I settle to the couch and fiddle with my fingers. A year ago we'd be huddled in a cigarette haze, but Deb quit for the New Year, so the smoking light is out. Women can do that. Just quit, boom, my mom years ago, my wife, her friends, now Deb. I smoke twice as much to pick up the slack.

"Lookit Petric! Jesus," she waves at the suits milling around the crime scene. "Hey Moe, the leather jacket thing has been done to death."

Deb's into the murder and mayhem and she knows all the cops by name. From the television, I have to assume.

"I don't know Deb. Broad daylight? Sounds like maniac either way."

She pokes her glasses up her nose. "Gypsies would be my bet."

"But why *not* some wacko? The hills are crawling with them."

"Naaah," she waves me off. "People just want to think that. Makes 'em feel like their own crummy lives are together, you know?" Deb still talks like a junkie, though she hasn't used for years. "Look at all the people livin' around here, jammed in like a freakin' parking lot. I'm amazed ten or twelve of 'em don't go off a day! Hah!"

She has a point. I wanted to shoot the guy in front of me on the drive over.

"Gypsies," she says again. "That's their style. Vendetta. Wait a decade or two then even the score. You'll see."

"Gypsies are a problem?"

"Hah! Take a peek across the street. You ever see seven people living in a trailer?"

"I think they're Mexicans?"

"Too tall for Mexicans."

I take a peek through the Venetian blinds, four Mexicans playing cards under the awning.

"I see what you mean. Better hide the children."

That gets her laughing until something seizes up and then she's locked to the armrests eyeballs bulging. As usual, I pretend not to notice.

"When are you coming up my way again?" I ask, hoping to finagle a future delivery. "Nice up in Lambertville this time of year, Deb."

"Oh man, Mary's got a bug about the dykes up there. Thinks they're snooty or something. That bunch? Hah! I could tell you stories."

"Tell me one."

She just smiles. "Yeah, that's all I'd need."

Deb's led a hard life and now she's paying for it. Bad back, bad knees, bad ticker. The vials on her kitchen counter run three rows deep. I met her six years ago through the dykes in Lambertville. I could listen to her all day long.

"Maybe I will take a drive up one of these days," she says, almost to herself.

"Atta girl. I'll take you to lunch."

"Yeah, maybe I will."

And we let it go. The news has ended and there's a soap opera on. One I've never seen before. The chicks are really slutty and there's a lot of rough stuff, not like Andree's soaps where nothing ever gets resolved.

"What show is this, Deb?"

"I thought you knew."

"Me?"

She shrugs. "We watch it every time you come over."

"We do?" Now that she mentions it, the sluts do look familiar.

"I thought you liked it," she waves off the TV. "Hell, I don't watch that crap. Haven't you heard? Television is a wasteland, man."

This is a revelation. The Deb I know would watch a test pattern if they still had test patterns. We watched the girl with no face right here on Oprah.

"We'll turn it off," I punch remote buttons to no avail. "Pretend I'm not here. Let's see what you do all day."

"Dream on, pervert."

On the screen the whoriest of the females dumps a pitcher of water on the bimbo with the big tits. I must catch the name of this show.

"How's the real estate business?" Deb asks me.

"Nothing's doing I don't think I'm cut out."

"I hear the wife's setting the world on fire."

"Yeah well, it's in the luck of the draw. My luck is all bad."

True enough. I've been in the office when Andree's

on the floor and the phones never stop ringing, buyers backed out the door. When I'm on everyone stays away, the phones so quiet I have to check to see they're working. You can't make someone come in and buy a house, but flipping the "Closed" sign around might be a step in a direction. The other agents shun me. My shifts are down and Andree outsells me five to one.

"How about the meat rack?" Deb asks. "You still tending bar?"

I feel myself blush. "They let me go. I don't think I'm cut out."

"You keep plugging though," she pats my hand, "That's good. Something's gonna happen, you wait."

Better be soon. I'll be 58 in a month and the lungs are really rattling.

"Bartending wasn't like I thought it would be," I tell her. "They really run you ragged."

"Tell me about it. I worked at Clancy's for six years. A real bucket of blood, that Clancy's."

Biker bar on Route 1, I wouldn't go there on a bet. The place where I worked made you wear a bow tie. They canned me after three days.

"I'll bet you were a natural, Deb. What made you give it up?"

"I couldn't hump it like I used to, you know... after the stabbing."

Like I said, a hard life. Besides the run-through at Clancy's she's got a bottle opener divot between her shoulder blades and a bullet hole above her collarbone. More like a dent, the bullet hole, but I can fit my finger to the first knuckle. A wild child, Deb, though you wouldn't know it to look at her. I wouldn't anyway. To me she looks like the dotty old aunt on your dad's side of the family, something about the glasses... or something.

I feel a rumble through the floor and seconds later a train clatters past, freight out of Trenton, ten minutes easy. We watch the whorey chick talking on the phone, the guy with the moustache talking on the phone, then six commercials and a station break without hearing a word. I slip outside to grab a smoke. Valley Park West, one of the older "mobile home communities", big trees, little lawns. The cars parked around don't make the high end, but the trailers are trim and a sign at the entrance reads "Motorcycles Forbidden". A nice touch, I've always thought.

I walk around working out the kinks. Deb and Mary Anne have flowers around the base of their trailer and the lawn is clipped and lush. Like most of the residents the girls have too many cutesy decorations, but they change with the season and I've grown attached to them. I circle Deb's car in the driveway. A long saggy cobweb runs from the dash to the steering wheel. The inspection sticker is three months overdue.

Whatever's going on, I don't want to know.

The train finally passes and the silence is a blessing. I smoke another smoke, pacing their patch of Whosit street. The sun feels good on my face and the breeze smells of cut grass. The Mexicans pay me no mind.

"Hey, I made lemonade," Deb shouts through the screen door.

Lemonade! For a second I'm twelve years old and just home from a double header.

"Don't drink so fast," she smacks me on the arm. "You'll make yourself sick."

"Glug-glug-glug—gaaaaffhuffa huffa, huffa...."

"And that's real sugar, too. I don't go for those watchamacallits."

"Gee mom, you're the greatest," I kiss the top of

her head. Deb comes all the way up to my shoulder.

"You know, I told Dot you were coming around today," she settles into a kitchen chair. "I guess she can't be bothered getting her fat ass over here."

Dot Darling, another of the sisterhood. Anymore I got dykes coming and going.

"I'll stop in on my way out. What's up with her?"

"She's retiring from the juvee center at the end of the year. I don't know how she does it, working with those little bastards."

"Aaah, you don't know. Maybe it's not that hard."

Deb snorts. "Last year they stole her car and used it to stick up three gas stations. One of the little pricks puked inside."

"They back in juvee?"

Deb gives me a sly smile. "Yep."

I pity the fools.

Outside I hear Mary Anne pull in the driveway. Mare's the girl with the goods, home at four just like clockwork. We hear the van door slide open and grocery bags snapping, but we're too damn lazy to lend her a hand.

"Hey youse," she shoulders through the door and hoists the bags onto the kitchen counter. "Did she dump the water on her head yet?"

"Just missed it," I tell her. "Academy Award, hands down."

"They don't give Academy awards for soaps."

"Whatever they give them, hands down."

"Damn! I shoulda ran the light on Street Road. Hey Snooks."

"Hey Babe," Deb struggles from the chair to give her a peck. "How's work?"

"Aw Jeez, it was swell. McClellan caught his dick in his zipper and Mrs. Wilsey set her hair on fire."

"Again?"

"It's loony I'm telling you."

"Well, it IS a loony bin, after all."

"Recuperative Center, dearie. Move your skinny butt, mister," Mare hip checks me out of the way. "So how ya doin' handsome?"

I bend to kiss the top of her head. Mary Anne comes all the way up to my waist. "How'm I doing with what?"

"I don't know, with life."

"He's not cut out for it." Deb levels with her.

"Still not working, eh? You can probably get a job with me emptying the drool buckets."

"Do they do drug testing?"

"Oh that's funny."

"I don't know, kiddo. I'm thinking I'm too old to break into a new field."

"Yeah, you're probably right. Loonies are a young man's game."

When the groceries are put away we file into the living room and squeeze onto the couch, me in the middle as is our custom. Mary Anne rolls a girl joint while Deb flips through the TV channels.

"Did they catch the stabber?" Mary fires the end then tokes up big time.

"Not yet. Petric's on the case, though," Deb tells her.

"My money's on the Russians. Sunset View is like the People's Republic."

"Gypsies. Mark my words." Deb nods emphatically.

"Heads up honey pie," Mary tosses my bag of weed. "You can pay me now or just leave your wallet," in reference to the other times.

"I thank you. Andree thanks you."

The composite of the stabber shows a thin, white man in aviator shades with a three-day growth and an earring in one ear.

"What'd I tell you?" Deb smacks me on the leg.

"He does look sort of gypsy-ish," I must admit

"Damn right! Ven-detta. Guy's probably halfway back to wherever they come from."

"Russia," Mary Anne gives me an elbow to the ribs. "Formerly known as the Soviet Union."

I'm thinking local guy with screws loose, but savvy enough to lose the shades, earring and three day growth. After that he's just another skinny, white guy.

"Hey..." Deb gives me a weird look.

"Come on, that guy's half my age!"

Now they're both looking at me and edging away and I'm retracing my steps to assure myself.

"Not funny, guys. Come on."

"Don't worry," Mary Anne takes the joint from my hand. "They won't get a thing out of us."

"Dude's gotta do what he's gotta do," Deb flips to women's basketball. Women's basketball is where I draw the line.

"Where do you think you're going?" Mary Anne pinches me with a roach clip.

"Prior commitments. Gotta run." I gather up my stuff and give them each a goodbye kiss.

"Good luck with the road blocks," Deb actually tousles my hair.

"You sure you got everything?" Mary Anne walks me to the door. "Dope? Wallet? Knife?"

I love them like sisters, but they really are creeping me out.

Dot's van is in the driveway but when I knock no one answers. I knock harder and wait for a while. At 5' and

320 Dot's not one to dash to the door.

"Whatchoo want?" she pops her head out the bedroom window.

"Hey darlin' I've come to brighten your day."

"How do I know you ain't the slasher? God damn white people got somethin' wrong with them."

Dot, who is black, was my connection for three years until she moved to Delaware to escape the trains. Delaware didn't last long, but by the time she moved back new bonds had been forged. It takes even longer for her to make it to the door now than it did then, the knees being what they are.

"Look at you!" she stands in the doorway with her hands on her hips. "Ain't hardly nothing left of you, boy! What, you got cancer?"

"Aw Jesus–"

"Cause I know you got somethin' Come in here, let me make you a sandwich."

"Just for a minute. I gotta pick Andree up at the real estate office."

"Get in here," she grabs my arm and yanks me inside. "That girl ain't feeding you right."

Dot's trailer is cool and dark and it takes my eyes a moment to adjust. There's an air conditioner groaning in the window and a pair of cats curled on the sofa. The TV is on, of course, and I hear wild laughter from some studio audience.

"Whatchoo want on this," she calls from the kitchen.

"What is it?"

"Never mind what it is. It's a sandwich."

She returns to the table, sets it down in front of me and hands me a paper towel. I peel the bread back for a peek but Dot slaps my hand away.

"Don't be playin' with your food."

"It's good," I chew with enthusiasm. "What is it?"

"Headcheese," she lowers herself into the chair opposite. "My aunt sends it up from South Carolina."

I force it down with considerable effort. "Headcheese? Isn't that... stomach lining?"

"You thinking of tripe. Got somma that too," she starts to get up again but I grab her hand.

"No, this is plenty. Umm-umm," I take another smaller bite and swallow it whole.

"Gotta feed yo man if you wanna keep him happy. I'm gonna give that girl a piece of my mind."

As if that would ever happen. Andree and Dot go back farther than me and either of them.

"You want a bite?" I push the other half of my sandwich over but she pushes it back.

"Not me. I seen how they make it once and I couldn't eat for a week."

The phone rings but Dot makes no move to get it.

"Deb tells me you're retiring."

"Don't you mention that white trash bitch in my house. Here she steals my best customer then expects me to trot down there and say hello?"

"Get out! I was your best customer? Come on, there must be somebody toking more than me."

"Nobody who can pay," Dot's eyes light up the room. "Why you think it took me so long to move to Delaware? Hell that was fixed income, tax free! Oh yeah, I knew there'd be trouble when those two moved in here."

Ignoring the fact that they moved in a decade ago and charge me less than Dot ever did.

"It's just business Dot, nothing personal."

"Don't load that Corleone crap on me. I'll scratch her fucking eyes out."

Ignoring the fact that Dot is godmother to Mary Anne's daughter or that Deb once fibrillated Dot back from wherever she was going. They bitch back and forth, but they're in each other's will and someday they'll share adjoining plots.

"That train still bothering you?" I change the subject.

"Not so much anymore. One of the two good things about getting old? Hearing loss."

"What's the other?"

"You can remember when it was different."

"You can?"

"Oh," she holds up a finger, "and you don't have to worry about getting knocked up."

The thing about my Valley West girls, they talk the dyke talk but carnally, they're all over the map.

Dot pulls out the cards and we play a little rummy, just enough to dish all the dirt. She wins every hand, laughing that big, Aunt Jemima laugh. I finish my sandwich and leave her some reefer. What headcheese is, remains unclear.

When stoned I am the consummate driver. I mind the speed limit, maintain safe distances, signal my intentions and always remember to buckle up. But I'm not kidding myself. What I lack in motor coordination and reaction time, I make up for in caution. I am kind, courteous and deferential to a fault. My mirrors are perfectly positioned and my hands are locked at ten and two.

When I'm stoned, my attention is perfectly divided between driving and pondering the unanswerable questions. I'm attuned to each rpm, every strain of motorized intonation. At the same time, suspended in the flow of traffic, I'm free to explore all levels of introspection, my childhood, my failed career, the meaning of life and permutations of death. Sometimes it all makes sense. There's a method to the madness that's vital yet tangential, applying to everything and nothing, a metaphysical equation beyond calculation, an intrinsic dynamic that drives the whole show. Oh yes, I can take these things to ridiculous lengths.

Or I can listen to the radio. Often I do all three at once. Like now, negotiating a lane change while listening to Bartok while contemplating the lunacy of life without health insurance. The guy to my right speeds up just as I speed up, unintentionally, I'm sure, but forcing me to counter with a drop in speed, a quick check of the mirrors and a signal left. Oboes and whatnot twine around each other to no discernible melody. House in hock, blood pressure spiking, life going up in cigarette smoke, when stoned my brain soaks up stimulus, processing information through the spectrum of emotions. And since almost anything is of interest, it's a self-sustaining state of mind. Beemer, British, envy, Bartok, Hungarian, composer, cardiac, pulmonary, ambivalence. Three lines of thought framed in acute self-awareness, an extended glimpse into the working mind... which would make four things.

I tongue a hunk of headcheese from a rear molar. Five things.

A mile to the Lambertville exit, I scan each overpass for idlers. Drop a brick through your windshield and its lights out forever. The radio guy tells me Bartok's later years were marked by "spiritual isolation and abject poverty." My heart goes out to the guy. I read somewhere that 50% of smokers do not succumb to cancer. To quit only to die of something else strikes me as perverse.

Crossing over the river I drift off on a familiar theme, a theory of possibility developed over a lifetime. In the end it's all about luck and endurance. Live long enough and anything can happen.

OK then.

GHOST STORY

Angelo's may not be the best pizza in town, but at a buck a slice, it keeps the locals connected. I'm on my way in when I see Joey G coming out. I try to dodge him, but forget about it.

"Hey Rile, how you doing?"

"Good Joey, I'm doing good."

"Christ, I haven't seen you since they sent up Hobbsy."

"Three years now. His mom just passed."

Marshall Hobbs, my former partner, presently serving zip/six at Graterford. For some stupid reason I think of Marshall when I shave every morning, always along the jawline, a flicker in my brain. I don't know what it means except those are good years going down the drain and somebody should feel bad about it.

"Me and Franny got a place on 58th," Joey tells me. "Nice place, two bedroom, we've been getting our shit together."

"Glad to hear it." I say what you say. Never mind Joey looks like hell and he and Fran have been getting their shit together for thirty years.

"Listen, Riley," he pulls me from the doorway. "I hate to ask you, man, but could you spot me a few bucks until my check comes?"

"Come on, Joey. I can't give you money to cop."

"It ain't like that. Franny's been sick. I can get it back to you in a couple of days."

I look him up and down. "Have you seen yourself lately? Your nose is running and your pupils are like manhole covers. What are you on, Joey, everything?"

"Just this once, Riley, help me out."

"What about Fran? Is she as strung out as you?"

Joey's face goes hard. "Forget it, OK? Sorry I asked. Don't worry about me and Franny. We'll get along." He pushes past me.

"Joey, hey!" I follow him outside. "Don't take it that way. It's just hard seeing you like this, man."

He pulls up, snot nosed and glassy eyed. "Franny's finished, Riley. Full blown, you wouldn't even recognize her."

"I didn't know."

His eyes go dead. "Me and Fran? We don't belong in this world no more."

"Where is Franny? Is she in the hospital?"

"She's at home. They were gonna stick her in hospice, but she wanted to die in her own bed."

Joey's crying now and people give us lots of room.

"Look, I'm sorry, Joey. I wouldna said what I said if I knew about Fran. You know that, right?"

"Don't feel sorry for me, Riley. I couldn't take it."

"Can I see her? Would that be OK?"

"It's hard, man. I do the best I can," he chokes back a sob. "Remember Riley, how she filled out that Maria Goretti uniform? Christ, I see it like it was yesterday."

I take his arm, just a stick through the thermal jacket. Their place isn't far and I brace myself, ten hard years since I last laid eyes. The house I know, the only one with a shotgun blast above the window, thank you DEA. I can smell Franny's sickness at the front door. The house is dark and quiet as a tomb.

"I better check first. Make sure she's up to it."

Joey ducks down the hall and I settle on the stairs. The walls going up are covered in photographs, black and whites from Franny's Daily News days. She was a dynamo back then, cruising crime scenes, one of the gang. I check the close up of Frank Rizzo kissing a baby, the kid's mouth caught in a circle of dread. The kind of shot Franny was famous for, prize winner from the word go. Then Joey came along and the rest is misery.

"It's OK, she just woke up so she's a little groggy," he leans to whisper. "Make a fuss, could you Rile? And don't let her see you wince."

He nods at the bedroom door, but stays outside when I go in. Oh man it's awful. Franny's barely a bump in the blankets, the rest is skull and yellow eyeballs. Not just thin but shrunken, tiny. She looks at me and wheezes a laugh.

"Riley Prentiss, as I live and barely breathe."

"I would have come sooner, Fran. I didn't know."

"Don't look at me, Riley. Just talk . You were always such a talker."

"I think I went off a little on Joey. Do me a favor and tell him I'm sorry."

"Joey loves me, Riley. I know it's hard to remember, but we were good together once."

"You stuck it out. That counts for something."

"Talk to me, Riley."

What can I tell her? How well everyone's doing? After burning her bridges at the Daily News, Franny severed all ties, shacking up with Joey in a West Philly flop. Every now and then someone would see her downtown but she'd slink off or pretend not to know you.

"I still have my Bowie tickets. Remember, Fran?

He cancelled and we got drunk in the Spectrum parking lot."

Her laugh rattles in her chest. "I puked into Joey's hands. Like he was gonna catch it all and take it away."

"I was glad they didn't show. I hated those things."

"I remember you'd say... want to get rid of all the assholes? Nuke a Rolling Stones concert."

Fran's breath is ragged and I can see the bones of her knuckles through her skin. I grab a chair and drag it over.

"How did so much time go by, Fran?"

"Joey says you're still with Kathleen. That's good to hear."

"You kidding? She'll never lose me now."

"I wish I'd been older... Who knows...? I might have gotten you."

Don't want to think about that. Back when I was easy to get and up to the eyes in my own cloud of chemicals. And Joey was right about that uniform. If Kathleen hadn't snatched me up there's no telling where I'd be.

"I'm scared, Riley."

"Hey," I level a look. "The Franny I knew wasn't scared of anything."

"What comes next?" She takes my hand. "What if all the crap they fed us is true? Hey Riley, I see pearly gates and I'm fucked."

"Come on, Fran. You know what comes next."

"No I don't. Tell me."

"It's simple," I stroke her fingers. "You wake up in a mansion and you're twenty-five years old. You have a big magic box and a smaller magic box. The big box is for the things you want that are big, the smaller one for things you want that are smaller. You use them a lot at first, but eventually you have everything you'll ever need."

"I like it. Oh Riley, let it be true."

"That's just the half of it. Everything is paid for. You can eat and drink as much as you want or not at all, as you prefer. You're never tired but you can sleep for weeks. Men adore you but you're fiercely independent. You speak perfect French."

"Make it Italian."

"Like a native, and the best part? Your time is all your own. You can write your memoirs and learn to play the drums. Or you can lie around in your pajamas watching TV all day."

"Will you come see me...? You know, after you..."

"First thing, Franny. We'll compare notes and see how far off I was."

"I'd like that. You were the one who was always nice... nice guy..." she starts to fade.

I try to see the old Fran in her face, but there's no bringing it back. I watch until she's breathing easy then kiss her cheek and whisper goodbye. The TV's on downstairs, but Joey's nowhere to be found. I slip two twenties under the sugar bowl and let myself out.

FALLING

Steve knew her, but not well. Their paths crossed in idle chat, odd bits of gossip. The block had turned over in the time he'd been there, townies giving way to the up and comers, pharmaceuticals, yappy guys going places. The men Steve could take or leave. The women were another story. Adele was the best of the new bunch, blonde, busty, half his age. She'd caught him ogling one day and gave him a playful slap on the wrist.

"Sorry," he smiled.

"You get used to it."

"Well... they *are* lovely."

"It's a consolation."

A consolation, her words, which he took to mean "they" were worth the bother. And what *that* meant was the subject had been broached. There was danger in this, they were both aware. It was the kind of exchange that can turn things, sometimes for the better, but hardly ever. Not that they were so inclined. Both married, both faithful, neither looking to take that plunge.

And yet...

Weeks since he'd seen her last, but that night he had a dream, somehow they were alone, Adele took his hand and before he knew it they were making love. Not fucking so much as melting together, steamy soft and all consuming. It was total surrender, body and soul, and when he awoke he'd fallen in love. Steve knew it was foolish, but his heart wouldn't listen.

"What's wrong, Steve?" Irene sensed the change.

"I, uh, must be coming down with something."

"Do you want an aspirin?"

"No, that's OK."

"Sudafed?"

"Really, I'm fine."

"You look like you just lost your best friend."

"My best friend is fine."

"I'll get you some aspirin."

"OK."

"Or maybe Actifed. Are you achy?"

Thirty-six years married. He'd known Irene since he was sixteen. They'd been through it all together, the 60's and the Village, the 70's and the Haight, twenty years bouncing from Key West to Mexico. She was so much a part of Steve it stunned him to think of her as separate and distinct, the one who made him whole but could live on without him. There was no Steve without Irene.

And yet...

He kept finding himself at the window waiting for Adele to pass. At night when his troubles circled he'd think of her to ease the strain. When next they met she was with her husband, good-looking guy, Jeff or Jerry. They were on their way for drinks at the Swan. The top she was wearing strained to contain her.

"Adele tells me you played some hoops, Steve." Jerry/Jeff squinted up from the pavement.

"No honey, that was Larry," she corrected him. "In the liquor store? With the beard?"

"THAT guy?" Jeff squealed.

"Back in *high* school!" Adele nudged him.

Steve couldn't picture it either, fat Larry Muncey knocking down a jumper? Not in this lifetime, any chapter.

"You play often?" Steve asked.

"Not as much as I should," Jeff patted an imaginary belly. "Maybe once a week with friends."

"Shooting guard."

"Right. We play over at the high school. You interested?"

"I might be," before Steve could stop himself.

"Give me your number and I'll give you a ring. Better yet," Jeff fed him his card. "Send me an e-mail so I'll have your address. Then I can keep you posted."

"Great," Steve slid the card in his pocket. The effort to keep his eyes off Adele was proving too much for him.

"Why can't I play?" she pouted.

"No girls allowed," hubby wagged a finger.

Steve could picture her jiggling all over.

"I'll bet the guys wouldn't mind," she read his mind.

"Sorry honey," Jeff shrugged. "Rules are rules."

First time out Steve broke his big toe. If not, the heart and lungs might have failed him. It was OK at first, the ball so familiar, the shot still smooth, but soon enough the legs turned to rubber and his toe hit the heel of his other foot. Happened all the time the doctor told him, a freak thing, but no less painful.

And that was that for Steve's basketball comeback, six weeks in a cast and summer settling in. He was on the front porch, leg propped on the rail when Adele happened by.

"I feel like it's my fault," she tapped his cast.

"I think osteoporosis was the deciding factor."

"Can I sign it?"

"I insist."

And then there she was, across the wrought iron table, perched in Irene's chair, leaning in, pen in hand.

"Jeff said you were pretty good."

"Jeff was being kind."

"No really, he said you were a sharpshooter."

"There was a time."

"Jeff's a real jock," she poised with the pen. "All sports, all the time."

"How nice for you."

"Yeah, right?" she gazed off. "I could march around naked and he wouldn't miss a three frow. Is that what they're called?"

Naked? As much thought as he'd given her bust, Steve had yet to picture Adele fully naked. Now that he had it was easy to arrange her in positions he favored. The sudden flood of images took his breath away.

She bent to write then looked up, so close he felt his heart flutter.

"This won't hurt you, will it?"

Steve let himself fall into those eyes, headfirst, in slow motion. Down, down, to the warm, tingly core of her being. And he knew he would feel the plunge for the rest of his life, and beyond, through the centuries, to the final crumbly molecule of *his* being. He really was thinking like that.

"What does your husband do?" he had to ask.

"Drug rep," Adele tapped his cast with the pen. "Jeff's a Merk man."

"Sounds," he paused for effect, "lucrative."

"He gets to make a pile. I get to be by myself."

Steve shuddered at the thought.

"You're always home, Steve. What do you do?"

"I'm in publishing." His stock answer, the one that begged the question,

"You write?"

"Only when I have to."

Why was he doing this? These half-assed comebacks he'd agonize over for the rest of the day. Steve looked at his fingers then looked to Adele.

"Did anyone ever tell you you look like Merle Oberon?"

She scrunched her eyes. "Isn't she an actress?"

"Movie star. There's a difference. Or there was once."

Adele plopped back in Irene's chair and whispered the name.

"Irish Indian," he added. "Originally O'Brien."

"She was beautiful?"

Steve nodded. "She was that."

Silence stretched, warm and sweet and Steve wished they could sit there forever. He was fooling himself, he knew, but nothing had felt this right in years. A minute later Irene pulled up with a car full of groceries.

"Here, let me help with those," Adele pushed from the chair and Steve felt the air go out of him.

Only when I have to? Jesus, just what sort of image was he trying to project here? He didn't give enough thought to his image anymore. But then he didn't give enough thought to *women* anymore. Sex, sure, but not real women and what they might offer.

Steve tossed and turned and tortured himself. Irene's timing, Christ! Driving up like the cavalry before Adele could sign his cast, blindsiding them before he could dazzle her with tales of the writer's life, artist in residence. She'd probably forgotten all about it, Irene sneaking up on them like that. Damn her!

And Steve really *was* a writer. With an agent and a by-God Google blurb buried in there somewhere. So he hadn't been published in a while. He'd dropped out of the game to write a novel. In three years he'd written three. And yeah, it took nine months to draw a pass on all three. And OK, the rejections were effusive, but you've probably made your literary mark when your agent tells you to give it a break. Steve tried not to be bitter, but five years was a chunk at this late stage. Irene came into some money but not enough to coast to the finish. He'd be sixty soon with no job skills and all the bad habits. He spent his nights thinking about it, but not in the way of solving a problem, more an exercise in numbing dread.

Of course Adele knew none of this. Steve convinced himself she would recall their conversation, if not right away the next time she noticed he was always home. She might even Google him, though good luck with that. No one had reached those cyber depths except Steve himself. A shame, too, the entry took you to a magazine website, his picture and bio. Not a bad picture either. His hair was longer then.

"Steve?"

"Huh?"

"Can't sleep?"

"I keep thinking about... that little cabin we used to rent in Tahoe. Remember?"

"Umm," Irene turned into him. "You could see the whitecaps on the lake."

"We hadn't seen snow in years."

Irene burrowed under his arm. "What were you really thinking about?"

Jesus.

She was wearing a Notre Dame t-shirt and a baseball cap, trailing an overweight Lab on a leash.

"Hi Steve,"

"Hey Adele. Who's your friend?"

"This is Schlomo," she pulled up. "Jeff's brother came down from Boston."

"Great dog," Steve bobbed his head. In fact, he loathed Labs. And yet they were everywhere, fat and slobbery or scabbed in allergies.

"If he doesn't get his walk he shits in the fireplace," Adele wrinkled her nose. Her breezy way threw him. He would never have gotten near the subject.

"Where do you walk him?"

"Down the towpath. I'd ask you to join us, but..." she eyed the cast and Steve couldn't help wishing he'd broken his arm.

"I'll take a rain check."

"How's the writing going?"

"It piles up."

"I'd love to read something," Adele touched a finger to her lip. "I've never known a writer before."

"I might have a story lying around inside," every one, two of most.

"Could I?"

Steve soaked in the thrill. "I'd like that."

He was about to usher her into the house when he heard the hairdryer shut down, meaning Irene would be coming down to screw it up again.

"Wait here, I'll dig something up," he hobbled off.

Once inside he didn't want to pop right back out like he kept his stories handy. Even though he knew right where they were, on the shelf reserved for his works, a thin row filled out by portraits of the cat. He studied the spindly spines. Then Irene came clomping down and the next thing he knew the two of them were huddled on the porch, laughing and talking in low tones. And he knew he'd look foolish coming out now with his stupid story, which Adele would never read, even though it was one of Steve's best.

For the longest time he stood midway to the door, looking at his reflection in the mirror above the fireplace. The sight so unnerved him he gripped the mantel and heaved a groan.

"Hey Steve," Irene called through the window. "Give Adele the one about the dog."

His mouth opened but nothing came out.

"Steve?"

He heard a chair scrape.

"Yes dear?"

"You know, 'Tracer'? Get her that one."

Right! "Tracer", his last published story. So they were talking about him, his stories! Irene describing "Tracer", gushing, God love her. It would all come out now, Steve's offbeat style and oddball characters, his brushes with success. Let her go on, flesh him out a bit. Freezing up like that, Christ, what was wrong with him? His stunned reflection, as love struck as a teenager.

"Do we have a copy?" he slipped it from the shelf.

"In the bookcase."

"Got it."

"Tracer", a weeper he'd penned in a flu-ridden fever. Steve pictured Adele reading the opening line. What was it...? Oh yeah, "It was raining the first time they saw the dog."

Adele turned as he pushed through the door. He felt himself tremble.

Schlomo shuffles alongside them, something Labs do only in a dream. Adele is asking about the scar on his arm, the one that stands out on a deep tan. And since it's his dream, the arm and the scar are considerably bigger.

"A guy in a bar," Steve shrugs. "We had a disagreement."

"My God, you could have been killed!"

"Not likely. We were both pretty drunk."

Adele traces it with her fingertip. "You know, I've never met anyone like you. What I mean is... I mean your story..."

"'Tracer'?"

"I cry every time I think about it. A lost dog," Adele looks away. "What he must think, the confusion, the way you described it, like a writer."

"My single talent."

"Oh Steve."

He stares straight ahead. "Don't Adele."

"But I can't stop thinking about you. And me, stuck with stupid Jeff."

"Don't be hard on him. He's a kid."

"Yes," she blinks a tear. "I'm so tired of kids. I need–"

His eyes snapped open. Staring up into darkness Steve could still feel her touch. Was that what woke him, or was it his conscience taking exception? Fantasy was one thing, but this was delusional. And yet it felt so *real*, the afterglow still glowing. So long since he'd fallen in love, so different from *being* in love. The heart's secret shading everything, throwing off heat, keeping him up all night.

His small infatuation, his cheap thrill, not quite pathetic, but semi creepy and borderline obsessive, but wouldn't that mean it wasn't so small? And that tug of attraction, was it merely one sided? She seemed to go out of her way to see him. The feeling was mutual, he was almost certain. And every day it was getting worse, or better, if he looked at it that way, which he did sometimes when he was too tired to resist. And he'd drift off and just let it flow.

They were at a party when the word went around. Adele had called the cops on Jeff. No charges filed but she was living elsewhere now. You could have knocked Steve over with a feather. And yet, stunned as he was, he couldn't be sure how he felt about it. She was free, that seemed important. But she was also gone. She lived somewhere else and he'd never see her. Already that Merle Oberon face was fading into the real Merle Oberon and he was powerless to stop it. And it was silly to get worked up, but Steve felt a sudden, sharp stab of regret.

"Was he abusing her?" Irene posed the question.

Maggie Wells grimaced, "No one's really sure. She was kind of wifty."

"Wifty?" Steve blurted.

"You know, flirty?" Maggie waved a hand. "She was always coming on to the men."

"How is that wifty?" Steve pinned her. "I thought wifty meant dizzy, or obtuse."

Maggie's eyes went wide. "I never said she was fat, I just said she was flirty."

"You said wifty."

Steve's little snit dampened the subject, but later, at home.

"So, what's with you and Maggie?"

"Come on, Irene, she was talking out her ass, as usual."

"It was in the papers, Steve. Police blotter. What's the difference?"

"The difference is I liked those people. Her."

"Hmmmm."

"Oh stop it. How come I didn't know about this?"

"Because you never talk to anyone," Irene yelped. "You float around in your own little world and nobody knows how to get there from here."

"You're supposed to keep me apprised."

"And don't forget we're meeting Sam and Elaine at the Candlewick tomorrow."

"Aww, Jesus!"

"Just keeping you apprised."

Clam Night, all you can eat with the TVs flashing NASCAR and the whoopers settled in. They had to wait a while for a booth, twenty minutes, in fact, long enough for the small talk to sputter, between Sam and Steve anyway, the women blabbing just to spite them. Steve was too distracted to socialize. He wanted to get away, think about what had happened, the love light going out like that. Was there something he could do? If so, would he do it?

And later that night, wide-awake in bed, feeling Adele's absence as he felt her presence, Steve tried to reason with himself. The girl was trouble. Her marriage was a wreck and the women had their claws out. Flirty? The notion stung him. Was he in her heart or just on the list? What killed him was he'd always wonder. There was no way to know without calling down a shit storm.

Flirty? Hard to believe he'd never noticed. He noticed everything about Adele. He felt they were in tune, aware of the others but in their own league. The men on the block were a sad mix, younger, sure, but pasty and overfed. To be lumped in was a blow, if it was true.

He burned to find out, yet he couldn't without risking it all. And he wasn't willing, or hoped he wasn't, as he could see from this distance and at every turn, what a monstrous mistake it would be. The sort of witless compulsion that makes men his age look ridiculous and he couldn't take that.

A week passed with no word of Adele. It annoyed him no end, the juiciest scandal in years and no way to follow it without being obvious. There was some truth to Irene's claim that he didn't talk to people, but Irene talked to everyone and her half of the running phone calls kept him in touch with the daily dirt. He knew more than he wanted to about the Weisman's burglary and the stray cat problem, but nothing of Adele *because* he wanted to. If he didn't care they'd be blue in the face with it.

Steve was in line in the post office when he heard it distinctly.

"Adele Skerrit? You're kidding!"

Maggie Wells and Gladys Glover, two spots behind him. He strained to listen.

"She's living over on Delevan Street."

"How is she?"

"We didn't actually speak, but she looked well."

He pictured the street, tree lined, little houses side by side. He pictured Merle Oberon in a hooped skirt and wondered why.

"Whatever happened to her husband? Jeff?"

"You didn't hear? He's in rehab. Somebody found him passed out in the house. By the time the ambulance got there he was barely breathing. Oh, and you'll never guess-"

"Hey buddy," someone poked him. "You're up."

He sat with the motor running, staring at the pigeons, the scraps of paper, the wide gaps of parking lot. None of it registered. It took months for the dust to settle now here it was stirred up again. Why would she come back? Crazy to think it was for him, but try as he might Steve couldn't help thinking it. If not consciously, by instinct, wherever she'd been had failed to measure up. And he took it even further, adding touches, making it perfect. She had come not to claim, but just to be near him, to fit in his life anyway he could arrange it.

"STOP!" he barked, drawing a look from a passing cart boy. And on the drive home, thinking about what he'd been thinking about, scaring himself with what he might do. Steve had never questioned his intentions, but he'd never had a reason to. He still didn't, so why did he feel like this? Like a doomed man going through the motions, lost in thought, driving too slow.

"You forgot the shallots and paper towels."

"Sorry."

"Why so much parsley?" Irene held up the bagful.

"I..."

"And no lemons! How do you make scampi with no lemons?"

"I'll go back.

Via Delevan, though he tried to fight it, actually wrestled with the wheel at the intersection. He knew the street from his summer bike rounds, narrow and cozy, old folks mostly. Empty now as he made the turn and the sameness of it startled him. He drove slowly checking each house, trying to picture Adele in it. And he saw so clearly every detail, the houses themselves, porches and front doors, the curbs, for Christ sake! He drove around the block and down again, slower this time, pausing to take it in, then left at the light and halfway home before he remembered the scampi.

He couldn't help himself. At least once a day he

made the pass around Delevan. The street was always empty, the houses, inscrutable. Maggie Wells was a nasty gossip but she usually had her stories straight, unless she was playing a game, baiting him. Not likely, but certainly not beyond her. He was at the corner ready to turn when he caught a flash in the mirror, a leg swinging out of a car, jeans from the waist down. He gave the mirror a tilt and there she was, turning away, crossing the street in that breezy stride, Adele, at last. He watched her take the steps to a mid-block brownstone and fiddle with the row of mailboxes.

The church bells chimed 2 AM. Steve listened to them snoring, Irene deep and lazy, the cat tailing off in a chirp. He saw the hours ahead as rows to hoe, a steamy slog through the scenarios, Adele, their reunion, cut to Irene, the guilt and so forth.

Shortly before dawn he came to a decision. Now that he knew she was back he would wait, let Adele come to him. Sooner or later she would find her way over he was certain, if just out of curiosity. He had no reason to be on Delevan, but she once lived on his block. They knew each other. He broke his freaking toe for her!

So he lounged on his front porch. Not all day but more than usual, late most evening,
sometimes into the wee hours. When inside he was at the windows, scanning the sidewalks, pacing from room to room.

"You're pacing."

"I'm restless, Irene. Maybe I'll take a walk."

"It's eleven-thirty!"

"Just to clear my head. I won't be long."

"Put a jacket on. And take your keys."

"I don't need a jacket, Irene."

"And bring a flashlight."

A flashlight, like he was some half-blind old gomer, Jesus. Though now he was out there it *was* hard to see. And he'd had a few drinks, shots in fact. And he swore he'd never do this, but here he was doing it, heading right on Union, waiting out the signal, four wobbly blocks north to Delevan. He saw soft lights through lace curtains on the top floor. It would be so like her, a garret lair. Night breeze carried the scent of the river. The first raindrops felt like ice and Steve stepped under the nearest tree, recalling a movie where a guy stands in the rain watching his lover's house. Only *that* guy was a slasher and he didn't have a tree, and the girl in the house was only six. But what really spooked Steve was the old guy out walking his dog, passing behind him, leering from the shadows.

"Looking for someone?" came the voice.

"OK, yeah, I am," Steve heaved a sigh. "And I suppose it looks a little strange, but I assure you it's an empty gesture."

"I see."

"It's just someone I can't get out of my head. It doesn't make sense, but it's all I can think about. Ever happen to you?"

"More than once, I'm afraid."

"I worry it's a symptom of something."

"Or a sign of life."

"You don't understand. I have a lot to lose."

"I understand completely."

Summer slipped by and she didn't show. In October Steve finished a story, his first in years, about a middle-aged man seduced by a younger woman. All of it true, except for the seduction, which sharpened Steve's longing, but freed him to indulge himself. The story opened on Christmas Eve, a light snow turning heavy as evening approaches. A few stores still open, a scatter of last minute shoppers bundled against the cold. Bud Decker is trudging home, a pair of gold earrings in his pocket, when he hears someone calling his name. He turns to see former neighbor and secret heart throb, Nina Varinsky, coming out of a gift shop. Startled to find themselves alone at this hour, on this evening, they share a few minutes. Nina looks radiant and Bud sees them as they might appear, lovers on a snowy corner, voices muffled in the stillness.

Sure the names had been changed and the events *were* fictional, but Steve knew Irene would see right through it. There was no fooling her. She could read his thoughts by the look on his face, by what he didn't say. So he never mentioned the story. And of course it was accepted by one of the tonier reviews, one he'd tried for years to crack. And though Steve knew no one really read those things it chilled him to hide it, making real what was make believe.

But that's what he did.

When a year-end anthology picked up the story it worried him a little. Irene was a reader and bookstore browser. By that time telling her would mean having to explain why he hadn't told her before. And there could be only one explanation, even if it wasn't true. And he had to at least consider the possibility that the story would launch him and that his big break would threaten his marriage.

But he needn't have worried on that score. As much as his story stood out (in his mind) not a single door was opened to him. No e-mail or phone call from, well, he didn't really know, some higher power, a behind the scenes player. Instead it passed into spring to nary a nibble. And though this filled him with a bitterness he could taste, he consoled himself with thoughts of Adele, his muse without a clue, his very own Nina Varinsky.

Still she stayed away. And though he tried to see meaning in this, a test of wills, it was more likely she'd simply forgotten him. The flicker of interest buried in the blur of living. He'd been kidding himself. The attraction was strictly one-sided. His story was more fiction than he knew.

The third floor was dark. The curtains were gone. Steve stood under the same stupid tree holding the book to his chest, trying to think what it could mean, aside from the obvious. That she'd moved out. That he'd muffed a second chance and would never get a third. Only last week they'd been there, the curtains, the soft light. If he'd done it then the next move would be up to her. Now there would be no next move. She'd never read it, never know his story... their story. No one would. Until he died and someone, probably Irene, put his works together, and that thought made him wince.

"Back at it, I see," the voice called from the shadows.

"It's too late. She's gone."

"He who hesitates..."

"Thing is, I can't explain my actions to myself. I hardly knew her."

"You're human."

"You think?"

Steve heard the rattle of tags and tiny claws click into the night. He turned to go, but something tugged at him and he crossed the street instead. Peering through the door he saw a cardboard free box under the mailboxes, the slim volume with "Tracer" tucked inside.

THE END OF BENNY

Maybe she loved him. Who knew with Kathleen? More likely she decided it was time to get married and Benny fit the husband bill. He was a merchant marine with a healthy pension and a habit of being miles from home. So, he wasn't handsome like Scott, or the Asian gangster with the silver Porsche. Benny had a house, a Harley and a cabin up the coast. His life was insured for a quarter mil!

I'm not saying Kathleen's mercenary. She's had higher rollers, but rich can be a bitch. The hot shots had to learn the hard way. They might be wiser but they're not as rich. Maybe its coincidence, but when the dust settles Kathleen's usually on top.

So she married Benny and settled in the Sunset where we didn't see her and couldn't even picture her. At first Benny bankrolled a hair salon—Hello Gorgeous—a Bay Area rage with the ego-impaired. Just the name spoken in that smoky purr was enough to keep the phone lines humming. Sadly, few of the calls had to do with hair and most went no farther than Kathleen's greeting.

"Hello Gorgeous."

Sigh. Click. Hum.

While Benny was at sea, Kathleen was faithful in her way. There were other men, to be sure, or a woman if she was feeling that way, but she never brought them home and she didn't let them kiss her. When Benny was around they fucked like monkeys, sleeping in mornings until the fog lifted. Kathleen learned to keep house and work the appliances and she closed Hello Gorgeous for the week, then for good. After years in the fast lane she became a housewife. Likely as not it was just what she needed, but those North Beach nightclubs were never the same.

I only met Benny once. My wife, Dinah and I rented a beach house for a weekend bash. Kathleen showed up with a short guy on a crutch with his nose in a splint. Some story there but the details escape me. What I remember is Benny taking charge of the fireplaces, humping by all weekend in a striped bathrobe with a log under one arm and the crutch under the other. Didn't say much, even to Kathleen, but late at night those bedsprings were bouncing. Could be she loved him. With Kathleen, who knew?

A month later Benny was dead. He'd been riding his Harley up on Twin Peaks when he lost control and hit a pickup. Make that double indemnity plus the house and pension and our girl was sitting pretty. A blinding bright side, if you ask me. Hey, I met the guy once. His freaking nose was in a splint!

I don't recall the funeral, but I know she had him cremated. I was there the day UPS delivered the ashes in a wrapped box with Kathleen's address in thick magic marker. The box didn't look big enough to hold all of Benny, but some of him would have to do. Kathleen said he talked about having his ashes scattered over the Pacific and invited us to join her in putting him to rest. We respectfully declined.

Weeks later the box was still there, on end, beside the sofa with an ashtray on top. Doubling as doorstop until she lost track of it, not what he'd wanted but not so bad. Still around, though not so you'd notice, turning up months later when the movers took the sofa. Coated in grime and tangles of hair, but otherwise none the worse for wear.

"Benny?" she held him in her arms picking at the dust bunnies. "Oh baby I'm so sorry. What must you think of me?" Then to me, "What must he think of me, Jack?"

"He's dead kiddo. He doesn't think anything."

"I didn't deserve him. Benny was the best."

"A prince."

"Finally gets his nose fixed and what happens? He breaks everything else."

"So what do you want to do?"

"Take me to the pier, Jack. Oh, would you?" she pleaded. "If I don't do it now I'll never do it."

I held a hand up. "I don't think so Kathleen. I'm no good with the dead."

"Pleeeeeeeeeeeeeeease," she hopped up and down to make her voice jiggle.

"It's a phobia," I told her. "Nothing personal, you understand?"

"You never liked him, did you?"

"He was great. With the bathrobe and the crutch? Ask Dinah, I was nuts about the guy."

"Give me your keys. I'll do it myself."

Not much chance of that. The last time she took my car she and a girlfriend skipped to Tahoe for a weekend. With Kathleen you take your lumps, but I expected more from Dinah.

"OK Kath, I'll take you on one condition. I don't get any of him on me."

"It's just ashes. The dead can't hurt you."

"I didn't want him on me when he was alive."

"Don't worry. I'll do the dirty work."

So off we went.

It wasn't far to the Berkeley pier, but we got caught at a train crossing and I started to fidget, Kathleen nodding the cars along, Benny lengthwise on the seat between us.

"Maybe this isn't a good time, Kath."

"Don't make me lose count."

A kid waved to us from the car up ahead. We could have waved back, but the train was endless and it started to drizzle so we stared daggers at him instead. The kid waved gamely, switching to the left when the right arm tired.

"We should have brought a spoon or something. How are you going to get him out of the box?"

"183... I'll just turn it over and pour him out... 185..."

"But that's not scattering in the true sense."

"Yes it is."

"That's more like dumping. Scattering implies range. You can't scatter in one spot."

"You made me lose count."

The kid was goofing now, grabbing the waving hand as if to stop it, swaying wildly to our indifference, unmindful of the gates rising, head first into the window when daddy hit the gas.

"So tell me Kath... what are you gonna do with the money?"

"Hmmmm?"

"The money?"

"Hey Jack, I'm still in mourning here. Sheeesh!"

"I just wouldn't want you to do something... you know..."

"Stupid?"

"Yeah."

"You don't have to worry. Ben's sister is helping me out."

"His sister? Look, I don't want to tell you what to do, but Ben's sister might not have your best interest at heart."

Actually, I *did* want to tell her what to do. There was a long shot running at Golden Gate Fields and rumor had it the fix was in.

"I got a tip on a two-year-old for the third race tomorrow," I came right out with it. "Going off at sixty to one."

"Rita says to put it in bonds."

"Rita?"

"Ben's sister."

"What kind of bonds?

"She says they're safe."

"What could be safer than a rigged horse race?"

"Listen to you Jack! Hustling a grieving widow. Benny had a hunch about you."

"Benny-schmenny. The man was out of his league."

We made the turn onto University heading west. Kathleen scanned the Keystone marquee, tapping a nail on the box of Benny. For a time she knew all the boys in the band, but a year had taken her out of the loop. Passed San Pablo and a trio of squad cars, over the bridge to Frontage road. The bay ran gray and choppy to our left, a wall of fog moved in at ground level.

"Pretty windy out there kid."

"We've come this far. I owe it to him."

"Me? I'd pick a warmer spot. Say, up on the mantel facing the television."

"Ben loved the water. You would have liked him, Jack."

"I don't like anybody Kath."

With notable exceptions, in a highly charged but unconsummated way I'd had it for Kathleen since she was a sixteen. Ours was an older brother to sexpot sister sort of thing that seemed always on the verge of boiling over. Dinah sensed my infatuation and vowed to kill me in my sleep should we cross that line. So far it's worked like a charm.

"What about Dinah, huh Jack?"

"OK you got me there."

Fact is I love my wife to a degree that is palpable. Our twenty-year marriage is the envy of neighborhoods coast to coast. I was as likely to cheat as I was to pluck an eye out and nobody knew this better than Dinah. Married to a one-woman man, as it turned out. Sometimes it's as simple as that. I don't screw around and I hate deception, but I am real big on steamy flirtation.

"That Benny, how was he in the sack?" I broached to the subject.

"He was a tiger, Jack. Pain and pleasure in equal measure," she gave a coy smile. "Or didn't you know I like the rough stuff?"

"He hurt you?"

"Never laid a hand on me. Benny just fucked your brains out."

"Not a pretty picture, Kath."

"He was from a family of sadists. One of his uncles was the last man gassed in Folsom prison. Benny said for his last meal he ordered a dozen steamed clams. Didn't eat them, just pried them open and stared at them."

"...!"

"I thought you'd like that."

How did Kathleen feel about me? Her conversation

was thick with innuendo, but no more so than with dozens like me. A big heart but hard to follow. The curse was you could never know it. She loves me, she loves me not, with Kathleen you were on your own.

"So, about my long shot filly. Say the word and I put a grand on her nose. Easy money, que no?"

"It's all tied up in court, Jacko. Becoming a rich widow is a time consuming process. But if it makes you feel better I can tell you this. If I had it, I wouldn't give it to you."

"Is this about Dinah?"

"No it's not about Dinah. Hey, I love you Jack, but I know you too. You'd charm the leaves from the trees if you could turn a dime on it."

It *was* about Dinah, the leaves in the trees thing, a dead giveaway.

"I just don't want you to pass up a sure thing, Kath."

"Well you know I've been pretty lucky lately," she gave me a wink.

It was still drizzling as we made the turn into the parking lot. A squadron of seagulls circled overhead dive-bombing bread bits left on the beach. We stepped out of the car and into a gale. The pier melted into the fog, those ghostly pilings thick as tree trunks. Kathleen grabbed the box of ashes and made her way across the lot.

"How far out do you think we should go?" I had to shout.

"To the end," she yelled back. "You can stay here if you want to."

I DID want to, but something pushed me along. The thought of her out there alone with the dead, unsuspecting me back here in the open. The main fright flick no-no's duly dispensed with.

"This pier is a mile long!" I screamed after her. "What fucking difference could it possibly make where we do it?"

She kept going, getting smaller, passing in and out of the fog like the credits were rolling. I hurried after her pulling my jacket over my head. A twenty-minute walk on a good day, in a headwind it would take us forever. I came up from behind and grabbed hold of her hand, turning her to face me.

"Will you stop and think for a minute? Look at it out there! You're gonna get us both killed!"

She pulled free but I grabbed for her shoulders, so she gave me a stiff arm and twirled away, running headlong into the fog, her laughter dancing in the wind. She wanted to make a game of it; some hide and seek in the cold and the wet. I didn't want to play in a very bad way, but staying there alone seemed even worse.

"KATHLEEEN!" I broke into a trot. My feet thumped the weathered boards, a pound of loose change jingled in my pocket. Wind cut through my clothes and I could hear my lungs rattle. I kept thinking I saw her, but she'd turn into a trashcan or bait shack or nothing at all. In less than a minute I was sucking wind.

"KATHLEEN!"

"What?" right behind me.

"Give me the box." I said without turning around.

"He told me the tide would carry him out to sea. He said to do it from the end."

"You discussed this? What are you telling me?"

"Benny was afraid of dying. He came from a long line of brutal, short-lived people."

"This is crazy. You know that, right?"

"Come on," she took my hand. "The walk will do

you good."

So we walked. I carried the box under my arm with my jacket zipped to my chin. Kathleen's waterlogged sweater stretched to her knees. Halfway there the wind died and the fog floated in roiling swirls. In minutes visibility was the length of a lamppost. If the power failed we were there for the night.

"Jesus, you can taste it," Kathleen took a bite.

"Easy kiddo. You don't know where that fog's been."

"Oh Jack, just look at it."

And as we did something shifted in the distance. A shoe scraped as a figure emerged. Tall, wearing a dark slicker, carrying a tackle box but no fishing pole. As he approached we could hear him mumble, low and growly, a black man's lament.

"The bitch be talkin' bad about me. Got to put things right. Time to be a man about it. Show the bitch what's what."

Stopping when he saw us.

"S'up?" a different voice, thick and unfriendly.

"Hi..." we left it at that.

"Got a smoke?"

"Sorry."

"Got fitty cent?"

I gave him my change and he shuffled off without a word.

"Pretty scary," Kathleen looked after him, hugging herself.

"Scarier yet, he's between us and the car."

"I wonder what he was doing out here?"

"I wonder what's in the tackle box?"

"Let's go. If he comes after us, you can bonk him with Benny."

We walked quickly, Kathleen on my arm now.

Foghorns sounded off the Golden Gate and the mist moved in layers as the wind picked up again. Right before we reached the end of the pier the fog cleared and we could see the city lights across the water. We stood with our faces to the wind.

"Well, here we are," Kathleen looked to me. I took the box from under my arm and noticed, for the first time, the thick seal of tape. I searched for a seam. There was none to be found.

"Just cut it, Jack."

"With what?"

"You didn't bring anything?"

"I wasn't even coming, remember?"

"It's just tape. You'll think of something."

Ten minutes sawing away with the car keys, a lame attempt to shear it with nail clippers, assorted slashes with the stem of my belt buckle and I was out of ideas. Kathleen worked an edge free with her fingernail, but the strip tore in a thin thread.

"I'll just smash it open." I started for the piling, but she grabbed my arm.

"Jack, no. It'll get all over. I can see it clear as day."

"It's gonna get all over anyway. You don't expect every little bit of him to go merrily out to sea, do you?"

"You know something? You can be a heartless son of a bitch," she let go of me and turned away. I wavered for a moment then raised the box like a club. Kathleen let loose with a scream.

"YOU DO AND I'LL NEVER SPEAK TO YOU AGAIN!"

"So what, then?" I held myself in the smashing position. "Walk a mile back to the car for a tool than walk a mile back? Count me out."

"Don't hurt him, Jack. He's been banged around enough. Just throw him in the way he is."

"You mean it?"

"It'll be like a boat," she brightened at the thought. "Ah jeez, that would be nice. Can you just see it? Passing under the Bridge for the last time.

"You got it," I heaved with all my strength. The box windmilled off and disappeared without a splash.

"Oh God!" Kathleen dashed to the rail. For a second I thought she'd go over and I saw myself just walking away, pretending it didn't happen, missing her madly but shouldering on. I may be heartless, but I wasn't going to die disposing of Benny.

"Be careful of that rail.... Kathleen, come over here."

But she stayed where she was forcing me, against every instinct, to go to her.

"He's gone," with a catch to her voice that might have been genuine.

"Yep."

"But no, not really Jack. The chaplain said he would live forever in our hearts."

"Some of us, sure."

"And if I ever have kids I'll tell them about Benny and he'll live in their hearts too. Even after I'm gone."

"Though technically they wouldn't be his."

"Oh... right. Well anyway I did what he wanted."

"In a sense."

As we started back I put an arm around her in a brotherly/sexpot sisterly way. Now that we'd done it I felt good about the whole business. Not our style really, Kathleen and me, seeing things through to the end like that. But now Benny was where he wanted to be and the tale would be added to the legend Kathleen. The time we went to scatter Benny's ashes and couldn't get the fucking box open.

"What will you do now, kiddo?"

"I don't know, Jack. I was thinking of moving to Hawaii. Get a place on the beach."

"Hawaii? Do you know how far away that is?"

"From where?"

"Anywhere!

"I think I would love it, Jack. I can remember watching quiz shows when I was a kid. Sometimes the prize would be a trip to Hawaii and they'd show pictures of the hotel on the beach and then a jet flying into the sunset. I used to dream about going."

"Kath, it's an eight-hour flight!"

"I couldn't believe it when they'd take the bedroom set or the Samsonite luggage. It made no sense to me, you know?"

"You'll be lonely in Hawaii."

"Right," she looked at me and snorted. "A rich widow with a house on the beach?"

"Dinah will worry about you."

"Dinah worries about me when I'm sitting next to her."

We re-entered the fog bank, keeping an eye out for the mumbler with the tackle box. In the absence of Benny I took off my belt and held it to my side with the buckle end down. What I intended to do with it wasn't quite clear, but it seemed to assure us and we plodded along. Through pea soup thickness and pockets of wind, the whole way back without seeing a soul. At the end of the pier we made a hard right and followed the lights to the parking lot. My car was the only thing in it.

"You OK?" I cranked up the heater.

"You're the best, Jack, bringing me out here. How can I ever repay you?"

"Put a C-note on tomorrow's long shot. I promise you its money in the bank."

"A C-note. You kill me, Jack."

"Or you can lend it to me and I'll pay you right back."

"Trust me Jack. I haven't a C-note to spare."

In the end she did move to Hawaii. For a year or two we'd get rambling letters or pre-dawn phone calls, but then the money ran out and she slipped back to Berkeley. Last spring she remarried. The new husband is six years her senior with a seven-figure income and a fetish for feet. We met him one time before we moved east and he seemed all right, once you got passed the imagery. In any event, he's worth a bundle and with the heart murmur and the coke habit he may be all the husband she'll ever need.

As for Benny, he never made the Golden Gate. The tide took him north and if there's any justice, he went bobbing by the racetrack as my long shot faded. Passing under the San Rafael Bridge, slipping past San Quentin and the Richmond refineries, washing up on the rocks near Lupe Santos' backyard Madonna, there to lay until Lupe came to pray. Momma Lupe was old, but she knew the score. What the tides bring in belongs to the finder. The box looked small enough to carry, but big enough to make it worthwhile. The rocks were tricky, but Lupe was careful, testing each step, taking her time. The box was sealed with tape, the address soaked to a smear. Her heart raced as she felt the weight of it, heavy as the answer to all her prayers. Back in her kitchen, she sliced through the tape, pried off the lid and opened the plastic bag inside.

"What is this?" she ran a hand through the sandy ash trying to conjure something of value. She saw words stenciled on the lid with an address in the city and a telephone number. Lupe called the number to see what was what, then ran screaming from the house when they set her straight.

The next day Kathleen got a visit from the Berkeley police. They had Benny with them along with a citation for the illegal disposal of remains. Where Benny is now is anyone's guess. Last I saw of him he was sticking out of a Nordstrom bag behind the spare tire in Kathleen's trunk.

TO THE VICTOR

Down here you have a choice, solid citizen or semi solid. But the semi side takes all kinds and once you're in it, things can go screwy.

"I swear to God, Vic. The man said Thursday."

"He said Thursday."

"Thursday. Nine o'clock, Fleisher Art Memorial. Look, see? I wrote it down."

"Look at me, Richie. Today's Wednesday."

"Get the fuck– Hey, where you going?"

"Maybe you can sit here for 24 hours, but I got things to do."

Richie's guy needs wrought iron and I got a garage full over in Gray's Ferry. He's a flake, Richie, but he knows people. I met him through a guy who had pool filters when I needed pool filters. Back when Richie knew what the fuck day it was.

"OK, OK, my bad, Jesus, wait up, will you, Vic?"

"I'm not here, Richie. Check back tomorrow."

"I'm sorry, OK? Jesus, it ain't like I killed the whole weekend. Come on I'll buy you a beer."

"Tomorrow," I beep the car door. "And wear something else."

He glances down at his Cluster Fuck T shirt.

"What, oh, my ensemble offends you? Yo Vic, I didn't know you were so..."

"Grannies have to look at that shit. Have some respect."

I leave him babbling on the corner, left on Eighth, across Washington. Some kid pushing pretzels at the freeway entrance, two with no mustard to spare the upholstery. Bear left for the Center City swoop, downtown looking major league. Exit at the Art Museum, Spencer Street, Hudson Productions, cruise for a space but forget about it.

"How much to park?"

The lot kid's smile is a dental nightmare. "For you? Nice ride and such, no charge, my brother."

"Serious?"

"Lookie here," he flips a wave to the lot across the street. "Cat says all the prime rides park with him. Now *this*," he sweeps his hand at the Benz, "is what I'm talkin' about."

"I get you, the competitive edge."

"Zackly."

"You Omar?"

He looks down at the stitched name. "Naw man, this is just his jacket. I'm Booker."

"You got a phone, Booker? Mine's dead."

He flips his open. "What's the number?"

I read it off. He pecks it in and gives it over. A voice tells me.

"Gilbert Hudson speaking."

I hand it back and slip him a fifty, tack it on Gilbert's tab. Not that he'll have it, but he'll want to get it. The next guy comes with a power drill.

"Do me a favor, partner. Brush the salt off the seats."

Booker smiles. "I'd be proud."

"See, the thing is Packer doesn't like you. I don't know what it is. The big mouth, maybe, just a guess."

Gilbert gets all red in the face. "You come to my

place of business to insult me?"

"It's not that far."

"Tell Packer he'll have his money Friday. Then I'm through with him and you, too."

I cross to the window and peek through the blinds. Booker's ass up with a shop vac hosing out the back seat.

"Where are you driving these days, Gil?"

"What's it to you?"

"My bet is you use the lot across the street."

"That's my business."

"Why is that? The guy gives you a break on the rate?"

"So what."

I flip the slat closed. "You should switch lots. Just a suggestion."

"I'm asking you to leave."

"Your crew, too. As a precaution."

Gilbert reaches for the phone but his heart isn't in it.

Back at the club Marty's telling Pistol Pete about Coral Gables, the sixty-pound marlin, like Pete never heard it before. Packer's in the back room watching Law and Order.

"And why, after all these lies, should the jury be expected to believe you now?"

"Get 'em, Jack," I sink into the couch.

"The guy was framed," Packer turns the sound down. "The perp is a cop."

"You know or you're just guessing?"

"Nah, they got two cops I never seen before and twenty-six minutes to kill. How'd it go with doughboy?"

"I don't think Gilbert likes us, anymore. You'll get your money on Friday and then he's through with us."

"And you know this how?"

"He sold his house. The closing is Friday."

Packer's smiles say different things. One you do not want to see. He settles back and turns the sound up.

"Your honor the prosecution is badgering the witness!"

"I was you, Pack? I'd want to stay out of the courtroom."

"I love that courtroom with the murals? My uncle was convicted in that courtroom."

"You'll ruin your eyes."

"It's educational, Vic. Frank Silver beat a murder rap filing the gun barrel. That one where the girl saves her own blood to stage a murder scene?"

"Yuck."

"Trust me, it works."

So I watch for a while, but it's in the middle and the show always bugs me. I've been to court and real lawyers bear no resemblance.

"All right, let me go," I grab my jacket. "Call me when you need me, Pack."

"You nuts? They're gonna read the verdict!"

Cousin Jackie, heartache of the family. The rest of us play, but Jackie's real deal, shot-gunned a snitch and served a stretch, walked out with no neck and a crappy attitude. My problem and I don't even like the guy.

"What's it say?" I trace a tattoo. "'Boon to–"

"Born to lose. And don't touch me, OK?"

"Born to lose? I thought that was Hell's Angels."

"Yea, well no one told me."

"Your mom wants you to come home, Jack."

"What?"

"To your old room and your wee little bed."

"Get the fuck away from me, faggot!"

"See, but I told her. Jackie's doing fine, got himself a place," I look around, bare mattress, TV on a folding chair. "Where do you shit, anyway?"

"Down the hall."

"So yeah," I move the TV and sit on the chair. "She's concerned. I told her I'd look in."

"OK, message delivered."

"I got another message. Stay out of southwest."

"What are you the sheriff?"

"It's called protection, Jack. Sooner or later you gotta protect them."

"Don't know what you're talking about."

"So OK, so now my conscience is clear."

"There you go."

"One more thing. Think of anyone you know, Jackie. Anyone. The last thing you see will be a familiar face. That's how it went for Uncle Pat and that's how it fucking goes."

Jackie snorts a laugh. "Who's face, yours?"

"No one knows the future, cuz."

His arm comes up with a cannon. "What future?"

A familiar face, the last thing you see, Jackie pulls the trigger and a flag pops out. BANG!

I stop for a snort at Pearl's. The place is empty so I pour myself a shot. Fucking Jackie, what do I do with this guy? Moves in on the bangers and gives not a fuck. Did I think he would shoot me? Pretty much, from the way my hands are shaking. Guys like that, you know they're going down. You just wish they'd get it over with.

"You here Mike?" I give a shout.

"Yo," comes a voice from the storage room. I make my way back.

"Hello Victor," he smiles up from his laptop.

"You even open?"

"On a case by case basis. The early birds know where to find me."

Mike is a pink little butterball with glasses and thinning hair. He opened the place after teaching public school for twenty years.

"You've been in the business for a long time, Mike. Anyone ever pull a gun on you?"

"Couple of times. Why?"

"Ever... you know?"

"Once," he rolls up his sleeve. "Kid shot me in the arm, fucking moron."

"How's that?"

"He shoots me then asks for the money. I'm bleeding like a pig, trying to fill his stupid bag and the kid panics and runs away. Funny you should ask, though," Mike turns the laptop my way. "See this guy?"

Thirties gangster, tall and dapper, posed in front of a pool hall.

"'Legs' Diamond, famous bootlegger," he taps the screen "Shot seven times in the span of ten years and lived to laugh it off."

"Yeah, but grow old and those bullets come back to haunt you, Mike."

"He didn't. The eighth did him in."

"Man, you're into this," I scroll down a gallery of mob mayhem, bodies in pools of blood, guys who look like they'd kill and eat you.

Mike shrugs. "My wife wishes I'd just surf porn like normal husbands."

Morgan shuffles in to remind me why I don't drink in the daytime. I leave a ten on the bar on my way out.

"Very nice," the guy paws through the wrought iron. "These are just what I'm looking for."

"We aim to please," Richie grins like an idiot.

"Now this is interesting," the guy pulls an iron section with a Star of David. "Mind explaining how this came to be in here?"

I look to Richie. He leans in closer.

"What is it?"

"What it isn't is salvaged," he waves to the prowl cars pulling in.

"Don't sit here."

"What, I know that guy from AA! He fucking entrapped us."

"You're a loser Richie. Fuck off."

"Aw, don't be like that, Vic. I'm as pissed as you are."

Packer's mouthpiece shows to post my bail. We leave the little shitbag in there.

What happened is Jackie jacked the wrong crackheads and the brothers took him out. I get to ID the body and it ain't easy, even with the distinguishing characteristics.

"Now what?" Packer taps his fingertips.

"Beats me. Tyrone won't take my call."

"Your fucking cousin. That won't sit well."

"They got their payback."

"Not the point. Our arrangement goes up in smoke."

"Nothing lasts forever, Pack."

He smiles that other smile. "Unless, of course, they still need protection."

Tyrone Banks breathes his last three days later. Another guy, Williams, turns up in a dumpster.

Some like the edge, or say they do, Packer, for one, always pushing it. The cops are all over us, tossing houses, rousting the club, squeezing every snitch in town. Media, Jesus, race war, drug war, terror in the streets etc. But Packer's a rock and I know nothing, so we break clean and wait for round 2.

Send the wife and kids out of town for a few days. Stick to the neighborhood and pack a piece. Don't open the mail. Stay away from windows. Shit your pants when a screen door slams. It drives you nuts, but you can't stop time and you gotta be somewhere.

"Not a trace. The killer wore gloves and washed the body with bleach. The guy's a pro."

"Come on Packer," I call from the kitchen. "Just pick something. I got the guy on the line."

"Garlic chicken. Small. And pork fried rice."

Eat, sleep, day three. And it's not like I don't have business to tend to and a court date coming up and a molar that needs work. And it's not like Packer isn't driving me batshit.

"So you drugged her and raped her and made her beg for her life... and then you cut her throat."

"Jesus, Pack, let me take a shower."

But the shower spooks me so I sack out until the food comes. Packer wakes me with the news. They fished Pistol Pete out of the river.

"Hey Vic, where are you going?"

"Out, before the cops get here."

I buy a bottle and drive south, rent a room with a sauna at the airport Inn.

"My God, what's gonna happen?"

"Nothing's gonna happen, Jen. Just keep the kids close for a while, OK?"

"Do you even know who these people are?"

"Look, the cops will come up with something. They always do."

"You're really scaring me, Victor. I knew life with you wouldn't be easy, but this is too much."

"Now's not the time, Jen."

"When IS the goddamn time? You promised me you'd quit Packer and his crazy shit."

I hang up, either that or take a beating. And the day, Christ, cold and drizzle, nothing good can come of it. Shitcan the meet with my lawyer and the collection rounds, call down for breakfast and hole up another day. Give it time, the shit will hit soon. Shower and shave so at least you look human. Watch them winch Pete's car out of the drink on the news. Check Sports Center against the spread and catch half of the Sopranos, the one where Tony's shrink gets raped.

Now what?

"Hey baby."

"Vic? Hey Vic, the cops are looking for you."

"Don't talk. Just meet me at the place."

"No way, they're up my ass here. You said I was under the radar."

"OK, OK. Any word on Pistol?"

"Pistol's dead! They made me look at pictures."

"Have they fingered anyone?"

"There was a big freaking hole in his forehead. I thought I was gonna blow my lunch."

"Diane, honey, listen to me. Did they make any arrests?"

"Want me to ask them? They're parked across the street."

"Could you?"

I hear her walk outside and tap on the window.

"Any arrests yet?"

Then a man's voice and a bus going past, then Diane raining curses and the phone goes dead.

Ventnor, my grand pop's place, sold it to the same developer who bought the house next door. He plans to tear them down, but they just sit there, phone books on the step, roses taking over. The night familiar faces came Uncle Pat bled out on the kitchen floor. Two nights later Jackie jumped off the roof. Broke both arms and laughed like a loony all the way to the ER. I circle the block and pass it again.

Raining hard as I turn in the lot. The lights from the Showboat melt in a blur. I check in on Jackie's Visa card, throw back a few then ring Tyrone's number.

"Hello?"

"If this is the cops I need to talk to Stevenson, 6th precinct. If it's Tyrone's crew I need to talk to Raymond."

"Say what?"

"Tell him Vic Rasko wants to deal. Tell him-"

"Tell me yourself, motherfucker," different voice, Tyrone's partner.

"Call off the dogs, Raymond. I'll give you Packer."

"'At's funny. Same offer he phoned in last night. Dogs for you."

"Tell me something. The guy in the river."

"What guy in what river?"

I turn off the phone.

By day three I start feeling like someone else. Thirteen messages, two from Jen, eleven from Packer, the last few sounding strained. I watch TV, movies, God bless 'em. Be nobody. Be nowhere. Disconnect for hours at a time. Things happen when you disconnect.

Check the news. Nothing happened.

Port Authority, funky on Sunday, lose myself in the New York millions. Watch the Mets beat the Marlins at the Gramercy Hotel. Grab a bite, walk the streets. Hit a bar. Hit on a barmaid.

"Hey cowboy, you always fuck like that?"

"No ma'am, I don't think so."

Irene, her name is. Says she'll stop back after her shift. I switch hotels as soon as she's gone.

I call Jen but get the message. I throw the fucking phone away.

The people who can help, they won't help you now. The people you trust, you can't trust them. Cut a deal with the cops and God knows what they'll hang on you. Go inside and come out in a box. Looking over your shoulder, dodging shadows, night sweats dying a thousand deaths. The end comes when you least expect it, so you expect it at every turn. Shit makes you screwy. I've seen it happen.

But things never go like you think they will. And with bodies popping up all over, the buzz is they haven't found mine yet. The big break comes when Tyrone's hitter flips on Packer. Then a witness fingers Raymond for Jackie's blast up. Headlines make it Stripper Takes the Stand. Only Cousin Crazy brings his girlfriend to a gunfight.

"They say it's better to be lucky than good."

"I won't argue the point, Mike."

"The competition gets convicted? That's stepping in it, Victor."

"Well bad luck has to count for something. Packer was losing it."

"Still, you couldn't draw it up any neater. And all you did was let the bottom drop out."

"The whole time I'm not even me, you know? Alone in my car, alone in a hotel room, two days, three, you forget who you are. And it feels good, a guy watching TV, how easy to just fuck it all."

"But you're too smart for that. You know how the pieces fit, where the others screwed up and what it takes to make it work. You can do what Packer and Jackie and your Uncle Pat couldn't. So you aren't going anywhere."

"Just history repeating itself, right Mike?"

"The criminal element, it's in the genes, like the gays."

I raise my glass. "To justice. In this particular case."

"Salud."

Tom Larsen lives in the Pennsport section of South Philadelphia, home to Mummers, Flyers and that screw you slant that made the city great. He and his wife lived in Pennsport for a decade in the 90's then moved away, then moved back again. Where the heart is, yo. For a writer auditioning characters, the 19148 zip is a casting gold mine.

Thank you to the Wapshott Press sponsors, supporters, and Friends of the Wapshott Press.

Kit Ramage
Muna Deriane
James Wilson
Rachel Livingston
Kathleen Warner
Robert Earle and Mary Azoy
Kathleen Bonagofsky
Suzanne Siegel
Phil Temples
James and Rebecca White
Richard Whittaker
Debbie Jones and Steven Acker
Cynthia Henderson
Nancy Lilly
Jennifer Bentson
Patricia Nerad
Ann Siemens
Elaine Padilla
Laurel Sutton
John Grigor Bell

The Wapshott Press is a 501(c)(3) not-for-profit enterprise publishing work by emerging and established authors and artists. We publish books that should be published. We are very grateful to the people who believe in our plans and goals, as well as our hopes and dreams. Our new website is at www.WapshottPress. org. Donations gratefully accepted at www.Donate. WapshottPress.org.